PRAISE FOR A.S. PATRIĆ

"The standouts were short stories by A S Patrić..."
Review of Etching 7,
The Age

"Terse, clipped, unemotional glimpse into
existential hell..."
Angela Bennie in review of *Best Australian Stories
2010*,
Sydney Morning Herald

"Talented."
Review of Overland 199. Owen Richardson,
The Age

"*Some Kind of Blues* is one of the most interesting
pieces on nationality, identity and the inner
dynamics of such things that I've read..."
Les Murray, poet and editor,
Quadrant

"A. S. Patrić will leave you breathless."
Wet Ink.

The Rattler
& other stories

A. S. Patrić writes in Melbourne and is a St Kilda bookseller. Alec is co-editor of Verity La, an online journal that is archived by the National Library of Australia. He has taught Creative Writing at RMIT and was a judge in the Essence of St Kilda Word Prize 2010. His collection of poetry, *Music For Broken Instruments,* was published in 2010 by Black Rider Press.

Alec is featured in *Best Australian Stories* (2010), and his work has been widely published, appearing in *Overland, Southerly, Wet Ink, Etchings, Quadrant, Going Down Swinging* and other literary journals. 'The Rattler' was shortlisted in the Lord Mayor's Awards. He is winner of the *SD Harvey Short Story,* Ned Kelly Awards (2011).

a.s. patrić

the rattler
& other stories

SPINELESS WONDERS
www.shortaustralianstories.com.au

Spineless Wonders

BN01164417

PO Box U220
STRAWBERRY HILLS
New South Wales, Australia, 2012
www.shortaustralianstories.com.au

First published by Spineless Wonders 2011

Typeset in Adobe Garamond Pro
Printed and bound by Lightning Source Australia

National Library of Australia Cataloguing-in-Publication entry

Patrić, Alec

The Rattler & other stories/Alec Patrić; illustrations by Miles Allinson.

1st ed.

9780987089724 (pbk.)

Allinson, Miles

A823.4

Spineless Wonders is a proud member of The Small Press Network

for my darling daughter
Summer Suzana Patrić

Gratitude & Thanks.

Firstly to my wife. Lastly to my wife.

To my colleagues and readers at St Kilda Readings, the best damn bookshop in the country. Special thanks to Will Heyward, a reader 'worthy of Borges', but kind enough to read the drafts of lesser lights every Saturday evening for years.

To my literary comrade, Ryan O'Neill, for breathtaking belief. To the *Inner City Writer's Group*, who helped me get this ball rolling. To my fellow travellers, for the ongoing feedback, and company on the lonely trails. An especially friendly wave to Bel Woods and Laurie Steed.

Thanks to Bronwyn Mehan and Linda Godfrey. Boundless gratitude to all the editors of Australia's literary journals, without whom this country would be a literary wasteland. You are the uncelebrated heroes of our culture. Thank you for finding the pages to make me a part of the great Australian story.

A final note of gratitude to my mother, upon whose lips the word *writer* was spoken in a different language, but always as a thing noble; and sacred.

Contents

Movement & Noise

The neighbourhood's children lived on the streets in summer time. A bowler would run up a driveway and fielders were ready to dive for catches on the nature strips or bitumen. Games of cricket could go on until there was barely enough light to see the ball. The boys had bikes and would ride in packs. In front of a given house you could see four or five bicycles, abandoned in a heap of tyres and metal tubing, silver spokes revolving when a breeze picked up — until the kids burst out of the front door and were off again.

There weren't many skateboards in that neighbourhood, but you'd be able to spot someone on roller skates. The owner of the local milk bar had bought his daughter a pair. White leather boots. Bright red rubber wheels. Sara was skinny and quiet but she loved to get some speed up on those roller skates. The boys rode past her like they were part of a gathering storm. They didn't stop to bother her and she barely noticed them. Sara's arms still grabbed at the air for balance but she was getting faster and smoother.

Her father came out of his milk bar late one summer afternoon. The boys were on the street, their bikes thrown across the hot bitumen. He walked over to tell them to pick up their damned bicycles and get off the road. They could be careless but he'd never seen them this disruptive.

Among the boys and their bikes was his daughter. They had gathered around her. Sara was lying on the ground as if she was asleep yet the road was so hot the heat was radiating right up through his thongs.

*

Sebastian didn't get off his bike. He had his hands on the handlebars and a foot on one of the pedals. He had been out riding his BMX in the paddocks, around the new houses being built past Taylors Road, when Alex told him about Sara being run down.

The ambulance had been and gone. A police car was in front of the milk bar, the lights on top of the vehicle turning silently. Without a siren they seemed like carnival lights but they brought out a hush from the descending evening, a single breath being exhaled for hours.

The boys had their bikes on the road but cars driving through the neighbourhood didn't yell or beep for anyone to move out of the way. They did u-turns and chose other routes as if there was all the time in the world.

Sebastian parked his bike next to a fence and walked closer to the owner of the milk bar.

No-one had witnessed Sara get run over but the police had noted the damage to her legs and head, and had told her father that the vehicle was moving well above the speed limit. Sara's father kept asking them why would the driver race away without telling anyone? Why would someone keep driving? Why just drive away? How could he do that?

His daughter might have been laying there on the hot road for minutes before she died.

Sebastian wanted to tell the milk bar owner that the man in the car would have been scared and that he wanted to get away without anyone knowing. Running away was something Sebastian did sometimes but he didn't understand the man's question. It couldn't be that simple. Not if it was repeated so many times.

As the owner of the milk bar, Sara's dad could often be found standing at his counter, leaning over an open newspaper. He offered commentary with a finger pressed down on an article. He saw terrible things happening every day and sold the proof to his customers, so it was baffling that he couldn't understand something as basic as a hit and run.

Maybe what he meant was that they could have called an ambulance earlier if the man had stopped. They could have taken his daughter to the hospital together. That hadn't happened and Sara's dad kept repeating his question as if he would never ever stop.

*

When Sebastian went home he didn't tell his father about the accident. Ivan got angry if he was asked questions or if he was told useless information or if he was distracted. At the moment he was sitting at the kitchen table with the radio tuned to a news show. He didn't ever seem to pay attention to it.

Sebastian thought about those silent police lights turning in the fading light of the long hot day and it occurred to him that his father didn't like silence. It barely mattered what the news on the radio was. Ivan just wanted to hear voices as though the house was full of friends.

Ivan had his shoe box out and a chess set beside it. Within the box were hundreds of clippings from the newspapers. Each strip of newspaper had a chess problem. Ivan dwelled on these puzzles for hours in the evenings. Eventually, he would reach out a careful hand and move one of the pieces on his specially configured board.

Sebastian opened a can of chocolate Quik. It had the foil at the top so he ran a spoon around the inside of the circle and made sure he pulled out every bit of the foil.

Ivan said over his shoulder, "Only three."

Meaning that many teaspoons because Ivan had seen five or six spooned into a mug in the past. Sebastian knew the rule, but he heaped the three spoons as high as he could and Ivan didn't notice. Ivan only listened for the three clinks of metal against ceramic, and let his son slurp while he drank the chocolate milk.

Sebastian's dad reassembled the pieces on the chess board to the original configuration of the problem printed on the slip of newspaper and started again. Often he did this all night with just the one clipping.

Sebastian turned off the radio. Ivan looked up and was angry until Sebastian said he was ready to play chess. Ivan smiled instead of yelling and waved his hand at the board like a magician.

Sebastian chose one of his father's raised fists and it revealed a black pawn. They began resetting the board — Ivan quick, stamping down the white pieces — Sebastian slowly, placing all of his black pieces in the exact middle of their squares. He loved resetting the board and his dad let him take his time. Sebastian adjusted all his father's pieces because some of them were almost in other files or ranks.

They played every day but Sebastian's progress was measured by how many moves he survived rather than victories. His greatest moment had been playing his father through to a stalemate. Sebastian still couldn't understand how he'd managed to draw. Ivan was probably distracted. Yesterday's game had lasted an admirable amount of moves (thirty-five or thirty-six) before Ivan checkmated his son with an intricate combination of pawns and a bishop. Sebastian was hoping to better that today.

The house was quiet, the birds outside could be heard in the trees. Sebastian could hear Jet barking from Alex's backyard, and that was on the other side of the block. If Sebastian's brother was home his music would have been playing. Derek locked himself in his room and played Springsteen or Led Zeppelin, The Doors or Hendrix, so loud sometimes the windows trembled. Sebastian didn't like his father's radio solution to the silence or his brother's noise, but he didn't want the house to be so quiet either. It was like that police light outside the milk bar today, turning noiselessly, except they couldn't even see the red and blue lights in their house. They just felt the siren when all the noise was turned off.

Ivan beat his son in twelve moves and then told him to go outside and get lemons from their lemon tree because they were having fish tonight. Sebastian was disappointed not to have survived the opening sequence. He wanted to reset the pieces and start again. He daydreamed of going one better than a stalemate. Not so much the winning part of it, but he liked the idea of beating his father at chess, and then refusing to play him ever again afterwards. That's what Derek had done. Now he never played chess, not even when Sebastian begged him for a game.

"Now!" said his dad.

There was a bundle of white paper in the fridge that Derek must have brought from the butchery. He'd been working there for years and had finished being an apprentice — though he never called himself a butcher. It was just a way to make money, and Derek saved every cent of it for the day he was going to get his license. That was just a few days away now and he'd already bought an old Mustang. He was still saving so he could paint it midnight blue.

Sebastian drained the last of his chocolate milk. He used the teaspoon to get to the undissolved powder at the bottom. He washed out the mug. If he didn't, his dad would shout at him. Ivan might stand up and slap the back of Sebastian's head. That looked funny in the movies but in real life it hurt a lot.

Sebastian shook off his wet fingers as he walked away from the sink. Before he could leave the kitchen, Ivan told him to go to the garage and tell his brother to finish whatever he was doing with the damned car and come inside. They needed to put dinner on and Derek had been cooking since mum went away. She was trying to get better so she could be their mother again but that might take another few months.

Derek would be in the garage. When he wasn't playing loud music in his bedroom he was in the garage with his tools and his car. Sebastian got a bottle of coke out of the fridge to take to his brother.

Sebastian went outside and felt the dry, baking heat of the day roll back over him. Strange how it could still be so hot, even without the sun in the sky. The heat was now in the concrete and bricks, the air and the ground. He yelled out for Derek but he didn't hear him call back.

Sebastian expected to find him polishing his car or under the hood doing something to the engine, but he wasn't working on the Mustang tonight.

Tonight, Derek was sitting inside the car with his hands on the wheel. He used to daydream and pretend he was driving, even just a few weeks ago in his dad's car, then he'd step out and get on his push bike like the rest of the kids in the neighbourhood.

The heat in the garage was intense and the driver's side window was open. Derek sat there with his hands on the wheel, sweat pouring down his face as if he'd been running for hours. It was falling from his nose and chin, and he was not playing his music. His Mustang made a dripping noise as water from its radiator splashed onto the concrete.

BOMBS

Smuggled onto the airplane, in with the luggage of one of its passengers, amongst the Sci-Fi magazines and dinosaur t-shirts, in a boy's wooden pencil case, is a lizard.

On takeoff the vibration runs through a man's bones and blood, intestines and organs, releases from his brain like apples from a tree, odd thoughts, things he hasn't seen for years, makes him wonder as he lifts one of those apples to his mouth how long they remain in there, unseen, but growing within invisible orchards… ready now to burn down to invisible ash.

A fire spread through the Elwood home, and though the family of four got out, the father later died of smoke inhalation, and his youngest daughter, just as sad for the cat, burned to death in the sunroom.

His blue shirt is worn through to the inner material at the collar, and he looks as if he washes his hair once a week, yet he sits beside her, not a breath away, assuring her of his success as a business attorney, he touches her forearm with his fleshy pink index finger, like he's intent on stopping her from turning the next page of her life, even if that's just checking the plane's drinks list.

Anxiety is a constantly fluttering, constantly settling crow on the bars of her rib cage, and it has nothing to do with planes and a fear of flying, it's more like a shiny black bird her mother gave her for a pet when she was a child, the initial egg forced in through a belt welt across her back.

His windows are clean, spotless, because of a bottle of Windex, but a bird comes in one day and crashes and crashes and crashes.

A woman's glasses broke, but before she bought a new pair she considered for three days and nights the possibility of contact lenses the colour of an open blue sky but this time her new glasses shatter, filling her skull with a new, breaking world of glass, and steel, and vast blue reaches, flecked with the perfect white breath of God.

The boy dives to catch a ball, (years and years ago, on a street, that happened to be in front of the house of Lester Ellis, when he was the World Champion), through the air, elbows before him, skidding on the bitumen, and doesn't cry—and is applauded by two men passing in an Australia Post van.

He cheated on her, so she left him, but didn't get to slap him.

It is precisely ten-thirty in the morning, Eastern Standard Time.

An accountant thinks he'll only ever buy wooden furniture when he discovers new plastic releases toxic gas, but the next time he's shopping he buys the cheaper plastic kitchen chairs because he's forgotten, and doesn't die of cancer, or a disease of the lungs, but by hanging himself from a wooden beam in the garage until he is dead, dead, dead.

She can imagine cat fur burning, and it seems worse than skin.

A man in the plane watches a child wearing a dinosaur t-shirt play a computer device, and remembers for the first time in twenty years what it feels like to have a loose tooth wobbling in his jaw.

Leaving Melbourne on clear blue skies.

Every night her mind is filled with dreams, with mythological pageants and intricate symbolical messages for her and those she loves, but she forgets and says that she never, ever, dreams.

The young girl beside him sits with a curtain of hair to hide behind, because her body has become a thing she is afraid of, or it's the rapid response it rouses in the men all around her these days; and he watches her, feeling it in himself, but treats her like she's nothing—gives her expressionless words when he has to ask her to pull her knees in so he can pass her seat—hoping he makes her feel safer among the landmines, that at least this one, by her elbow, isn't going to detonate with male hunger.

A cruising altitude of thirty-nine thousand feet.

There are birds, in a cage made of wood to resemble an Indian palace, with minarets and shallow mosaic ornamental pools, and they will die on the same day, though at different hours, because the humans, moving slow, blind and deaf to their distress, stop feeding them, or giving them water, and they are already so hungry and thirsty.

She grew up in country Victoria, out past the natural spring spas of Daylesford, moving from town to town, living for a year in a church that wasn't a church anymore, and learning in that draughty place how to keep the warmth in the centre of her body with a wordless chant.

A fine day, reaching temperatures of twenty-three degrees Celsius, or seventy-three degrees Fahrenheit, with strong westerlies building by the afternoon.

The boy is distressed to discover that the lizard has crawled outside of his wooden pencil case, leaving its tail in the hand luggage, and doesn't know if the lizard can grow another one or not, because it could be like losing his teeth, which were already growing back, or it could be like his friend's pointing finger, which got a centimetre cut off it in his father's woodshed, on the spinning saw, and will never grow back, even though it's only a centimetre.

There are dusty boxes buried in wardrobes, filled with first love letters and school ribbons and photographs, that will never be opened again.

There is music that is played and heard, and the recording devices lie about these things, making it seem as though an instant can last an eternity, and that the law of this world is not the final moment gone already, as it hangs, a tinny whispering, from fluff-tipped headphones, swinging from an armrest, playing music from the airplane's radio.

There's a message on an answering machine that tells a man that he is loved, and it will never be explained why it was recorded, since the speaker understands he is gone and will never return for his messages.

A woman lolls in her seat, checks her watch as others start their raucous chattering, their monkey-fear arm waving, and wishes she could have a cigarette.

She still remembers the cat's name, and she died and died and died in dreams, with lungs full of smoke, so that now there will be a fire full of her father.

When the flight attendant looks outside the windows she sees a clear blue world with a powdered white expanse of clouds—emptied of everything—but her daydreams have filled them with darting hopes and with angels kicked loose and free from broken hives, flying out to the Queen, mouths full of pollen.

The boy checks the time on his first watch, counting the little bars around the three revolving arms and calculating the time to be ten-forty-six and thirty-five seconds, thirty-six seconds, thirty-seven seconds in the morning, and can't decide whether he should wear it on his right wrist or his left wrist.

She didn't get to slap him, after the lawyers and their bowls of stale mints, their florid ties and their flat-screen television eyes, but what was worse than not getting to slap him was the business-like handshake at the end of their marriage.

The man with scars on his elbows (from a wonderful cricket catch taken on a suburban road), is not Muslim, not part of a global organisation of bogey men, and could have been the lovely man some fortunate woman brought home for dinner to her lovely parents in a respectable neighbourhood in a lovely Australian suburb, but he learned how to build bombs in the Australian Army, and life for him didn't translate as anything other than a world filled with monsters erupting from beneath his childhood bed.

She has lived her whole life, travelling the four points of the compass, pointing out all the exits, and has never discovered that her surname, in the Basque language, means *Snail.*

There is a hiss that lasts as long as an angry breath and then it's a roar with everything escaping, like he'd lived in a balloon his whole life, and this was bound to happen someday.

The bodies of a mother and child will be found in a few hours, the two forms driven with the force of the aircraft's exploding fuselage against the mountainside into one heap of matter, but it will never be known from these remains what the boy feels now, in the crush of his mother's embrace, her voice whispering love into his ear so that he can hear nothing else.

He thought there would be one early moment from his life that he would remember, or there would be a series of flashes, but he's never been able to imagine what it would be, and it is surprising that it's a Sunday afternoon in summer, watering the grass, walking barefoot, the sound of his girls talking and laughing as they play in the pool.

She's told her husband that she believes she has a soul but doesn't believe in God, and he's told her that he believes in God, but suspects he's lost his soul, and now they hold hands as the vibration is enough to loosen their bones from their sockets.

She ghosts through the house it took her fifty years to perfect, along the dark polished oak floorboards, into her kitchen and across stainless surfaces and hand-made tiles, passing beneath each modulated hidden light fixture, every effect-calibrated painting and knickknack on white walls, across black leather upholstery and its smell of luxury, through to the appointed bedrooms and luxurious linens and wardrobes full of her considered choices; all of it a living work of art, reflecting everything she was, and wanted to be—an exhibit perfected by her death.

There's a yapping dog, notorious for his persistent barking, who will be silent for a month, dwell beneath the house and utter not a yelp, despite all these strangers tramping above and around him.

And didn't her husband deserve that one ringing slap, for breaking the only vow he'd make in a life that didn't take promises seriously, (of course, no-one did), but there was the ritual and a priest who asked him before family and friends, asked him by name, until death do you part?

A son walks into the garage twenty four hours later, and finds his father, the swing in his hanging feet, suspended dead, dead, dead, from the wooden beam, a mask of flies like a butcher's curse across his father's face, written into his own, so that the son has woken, many times, with a suffocating mask of flies.

There are heavens and hells, but we don't get to choose, and it's one that is just buried in the soul somewhere, because he will see those Elysian Fields emerging through the fire, and he never would have thought tall grass endlessly rolling could be freedom so endless.

Behind her curtain of hair, even as the people standing up begin toppling, and the explosion releases flame right across their window, so this is happening, no way out, and death real, with the sound of metal tearing, and the plane sliding around, even then she clings to herself, arms wrapped about her body, and doesn't reach out for him, sitting there by her elbow, just another male bomb.

He was in his late thirties when he started having children, and in areas of his heart had given up on their possibility, truly let their hope die in him, but they came, one, two, and three— while his body was incinerated, the old leather wallet, (bought before all their time) survived undamaged and contained pristine pictures of those three daughters—all redheads.

It won't take long for snow to drift across the mountainside, to cover everything in a fine dusting of crystals, gathering on flesh and metal when they cool.

She watched so many movies, in which the yellow masks bounce down from the overhead compartments to dangle like rubber chickens, everyone screaming, rushing around, and things tilt and jerk and shake because it's all about cameras, but she finds it's nothing like that, most people stay in their seats when it's about to happen, wait, submission comes as naturally as breathing, as holding your breath, and they are quiet in the roar.

When the crash comes, the mask of flies lifts, scatters in a million directions, and dead, dead, dead, is the swing of the pendulum in the clockwork of lies at the centre of his father's life, which is not how the heart works, merely pushing blood to strict time, but is a double beat rhythm in the on-off signals of Morse code, pulsing for the truth: *more-love, more-love, more-love.*

It had been hazy but it clarified as his moment drew closer and closer, as the passengers lifted from their seats, falling back into them, began to trouble him with their noise and panic, he began to feel like just another man about to die, in no way special because he had made this death—his motivation as a bomb maker, that one clear idea of perfect clarity, disintegrates, and he finds nothing but clambering confusion that does not give him space to remember the reasons for his bombs, space for memories of who he was and what he had done, and why, the why is obliterated as his body explodes in a steam of blood and splintering bone.

There are animals in falling cages, with no windows to the outside, all in the hold, their deaths unwitnessed, but they have each been given a name, and were chosen in one way or another by an act of human love.

Behind her curtain of hair, she can't know how much he wishes he could protect her, and how he would push his own life in front of her death, instead of going down with her like an unexploded landmine, because what she doesn't understand is that some men are enemies, as she well knows, but some are of her tribe, born, not to raid and rape, but to offer protection, and they find this impulse, this kind of sacrifice worth every hope they've ever had.

She has trained to prepare for crashing, without ever accepting that a plane will crash with her onboard, but a flight attendant has air in her dreams like an alligator has river mud, as she finds a window and watches a rocky mountainside through the blue air race up towards the glass with her eyes open, a surprising love swells her heart, fills her eyes with hot tears, sweet in her throat, and finds silent release in an expanse of infinite blue whispering white.

Brief Moments of Interruption

Julian steps out into the light rain with his wife's umbrella. A walk will do him good. That's what his wife had told him. After a few steps, he still can't swallow, so he stops with his hand raised, the fingertips almost touching his larynx. He doesn't think it's another stroke. There isn't that feeling of unbearable complication at the base of his brain.

The umbrella's material is translucent and it has bright circles of colour. He likes using it. He feels illuminated below it and prefers it to the black one.

It's the kind of Sunday where it's more practical to stay indoors. Rain drips from the roofs of letterboxes, even when the weather clears for a few minutes. Newspapers are wet right through. Dogs remain huddled in dry spaces beside their houses, making brief forays out to the front fence when Julian passes.

The concrete paths are wet, though the puddles are easy to walk around. He decides on walking along the canal — perhaps all the way up to the man-made lakes in Elsternwick Park. Depends on how he feels at the turn-off at the golf course. There's something about the artificial lake that makes him feel desolate. The despondent swans and ducks are meagre and the water seems no more than an immense, permanent puddle.

He is able to swallow now. It's a question of not trying; not thinking about the throat too much and how mysterious that mechanism of moving saliva down the gullet actually is when it's not an automatic function. So much is not controlled, thinks Julian. It's when there is a brief interruption to all those functions that a person can see how everything works— perpetually beyond all conscious control.

He continues along the bitumen path that follows the Elwood Canal. The houses and apartment blocks are close enough for this watercourse to be part of a communal backyard. It connects a large section of the neighbourhood like the discrete spine of a turtle, creating a sense of community and inclusion, though communal gathering points are absent.

Julian has written a book called *Turtle Shell Design*. His wife tells him it's an architecture book. She tells him that the book says that a spine is barely required when there's a perfect shell. That book sits on a shelf, in his study at home, alongside many other books by different authors.

There is chalk on the path that's getting smudged by the rain. *Slow Down* it tells him in a long arrow directed the way he is going and to further images drawn on the ground by the hands of many children. It might have been the one very precocious, busy child, but he has the feeling that there have been three, four, or even five children from the nearby houses at work on this path. Their chalk drawings, made in reds, greens, yellows and blues, are of spaceships that resemble electric eels surrounded by starfish stars.

The rain hasn't done any of these images favours, but the chalk looks like it will last through one or two more days of wet weather. At the other end of this bit of street art is another arrow, pointing back the way he's come, and the same message, *Slow Down*. He can imagine the children on hands and knees, working at their chalk mural, worried about getting trampled by powerwalkers with tinkling iPods or dogs straining on leashes as owners come marauding through or helmeted cyclists with heads down, threatening to run them over.

He nears a bridge crossing the canal that looks as if it's from a children's book. He wonders what he would have thought when he was a child. Most memories have been erased with the short circuit. He isn't sure whether once-upon-a-time he would have imagined a troll living under the bridge. Did he ever believe in such a thing? His whole childhood has vanished in one brief moment of interruption.

He walks across the bridge knowing that he used to be able to analyse every part of it, from the size and type of the bolts used in it, to the technical history of its construction. Whether certain features were borrowed from a Japanese architectural fashion or a sturdy Roman archetype. It's just a bridge now that spans across a wide part of the canal and the houses on either side are waterproof boxes with families living within them, happy to be out of the rain on a Sunday afternoon.

Julian carries his wife's umbrella and crosses the bridge and thinks about how even the water runs through here because it was directed by human hands. He tries to imagine how many men have been at work here the same way he had thought about how many children made the chalk drawings.

Maybe he used to know that as well, but concrete and stone and steel suck in those kinds of ghosts. Julian's hands had made things too. It doesn't matter what he remembers or whether people passing by see the ghosts or not. Those made things are the memories of hands. The buildings he designed have recorded his understanding and his imagination and his passion. It's only in his own memory that things are put down in chalk.

There are bends built into the canal but it doesn't have the surging current of a river. It simply runs water from the drains of the neighbourhood out to the bay, overflowing at its narrowest point with this rain. The grass alongside is a flooded marshland. At the low water crossing on Foam Street, a car has foundered halfway through the ford. It stands in the middle of the road, locked and abandoned, as though nothing more could be done once water got into its engine.

He walks further along and finds a dead bird in the grass. He doesn't know what it is. What it was. One of those small birds. Sparrows or finches, canaries or robins—he wouldn't know how to separate any of them. He's pretty sure he never did. A small bird lying in the grass, soon to have all its secrets revealed by parades of ants. The wet ground and grass might keep them away for a while. As Julian passes he notices the bird make another movement but he keeps walking without looking back.

A few weeks ago he woke after a long sleep and something bad had happened. Julian doesn't want to think about it but he knows he can't help it. The bird reminds him.

Before the stroke he'd had trouble sleeping for longer than five hours but he now found it difficult to get out of bed after twelve hours. He could endlessly drift in and out of sleep, never remembering any of his dreams.

No-one was at home. His wife was at work and the children at school. No reason for him to get out at all but he heard a rustling sound. A clanking, clicking sound somewhere inside the house. It might have been going on for hours but he wondered what it was. Definitely coming from inside the house. When he opened the bedroom door, the noise was in the kitchen and he couldn't think of an explanation.

He discovered that it was a mouse, caught in a mousetrap. Neck not quite broken, and not entirely strangled. Julian didn't want to deal with it and considered calling someone to come and dispose of the half-dead mouse. The rustling sound of it moving the trap, back and forth, across the tiles was terrible. He got a shoe, and with his eyes closed, Julian hit the mouse in the trap. It didn't die and there was a fearful moment when he thought that he might have to hit it again. He threw it in the kitchen bin, tied off the liner, and took it outside to the garbage bins outside.

The dead bird reminds him of that mouse. The bird might not have moved but Julian can't help imagining those parades of ants arriving early and getting at those secrets before the bird is ready to open up.

He walks along the canal and when he comes to the golf course he decides he doesn't want to see the lake in Elsternwick Park, so he takes a left and crosses the concrete bridge and follows the road through the neighbourhood.

He knows he will miss this — walking through Elwood. It's been his home for over a decade. When he was successful he bought a house on Addison Street and tore it down and built something new. He remembers the unrolled blueprints spread out on his tilted architect's desk. He knows he used to be able to see his wife and daughters in those drawings.

The land Elwood is on used to be swampland, and it's the reason for the canal. Some of the houses around here are cracking and have sunk to one side in catastrophic millimetres. But the house he built is perfect. Not even the slightest crack anywhere. His wife is selling the house Julian designed, but it's not clear to him why. A young couple with twins are viewing it right now. They've been over once before but Julian started shouting at them.

He stops at the street corner of Tennyson and Byron. There are roads going in different directions, shunting vehicles around and through. The traffic can often seem as though it's careening and there are no traffic lights. Julian stands there a few minutes sometimes to get his bearings.

30

A car pulls up beside him, waiting for traffic to move through. The passenger in the car has his window rolled down and his elbow rests on the ledge.

"It's not raining," the passenger says. Julian realises he's still holding his wife's umbrella above his head and that the light rain has ceased. Perhaps it stopped raining as soon as he left home.

"Thanks," he says, and raises his hand. It's almost a wave.

The gesture is reminiscent of those made in holy pictures where saints offer blessing to the faithful. He's seen those kinds of images but he can't remember where. The name *Giotto* remains — a fragment of knowledge that he was an artist born in Florence, the first great painter of the Renaissance. Julian doesn't recall what Renaissance means anymore and the gesture of blessing, or of greeting, stays between the two men for a moment longer.

The passenger looks at the open umbrella and at Julian again, and just before the car guns through the intersection, he says, "Fucken retard!"

The Coultas Kid

I swam through the water as though I'd forgotten I needed the air above. Beneath the surface was a woman—gliding from one edge of the pool to the other. She looked as though she was born in the water. She was beautiful like something made up and couldn't be true. I followed the mermaid below because I couldn't help looking at her and feeling her move through my eyes; a dream for my wide awake mind. The way she kicked with her whole body—and kept kicking in a wave motion. Her running hair and rippling legs and arms all flowing. There had to be a spell she'd discovered so she could breathe underwater forever. It was a magic hook around one of my ribs and it pulled me under, deeper into the wide awake beautiful dream of the mermaid.

But my lungs hauled me to the surface. Brought me up spluttering. My limbs thrashed around me. Air got mixed in with water, and I was swallowing more, breathing it, unable to cough it out. Drowning before I knew that was even really possible. Going below the surface again, the light above getting far away. And gone.

The mermaid hadn't vanished into the blue water spell. She brought me to the side of the pool. Her smooth arm around my chest. Waited there at the water's edge for me to cough out the water. She didn't say anything. She watched me and when I was OK, she swam out below again.

I walked trembling, out to my parents who were sitting with friends on a blanket, laughing. When I collapsed next to my mother and told her with chattering teeth I almost died, she went on laughing. Ignored me as if I was too young to talk about dying. It hadn't been real for me either, before the mermaid.

I spent weeks thinking about it. Lifting the doona above my head and holding my breath. Reaching two minutes seemed a good goal, but every time, like the most precise clockwork ever invented, I'd get to one minute and ten seconds and gasp. I almost blacked out at one minute twenty. I learned to oxygenate my blood by breathing in and out deeply for a full minute before holding my breath and managed to get to a minute forty. Two minutes seemed impossible, but I had this idea that by getting there, maybe something could change. I would have moved towards some kind of threshold. I asked people how to train for holding your breath but no-one had any good ideas. Mr. Steed, our next door neighbour, told me about deep sea divers he'd seen who could hold their breath for ten minutes. He was probably making it up but I thought if there were such divers then they would be well beyond the impossible two minute mark I wanted to reach.

One morning I woke up with a bad smell all around me. I opened my window and breathed the air out there. Opened my door and smelled that the air was much worse in the rest of the house. I moved to the front door near my bedroom and opened it. Went to the kitchen, walking quickly, past my parent's bedroom with its open door, past the open door of my baby sister's bedroom, and turned off the gas top oven. It wasn't lit but it made the hissing noise that meant it was on.

I went to the back door and opened it. Breathed out there. I thought my parents would be happy I'd thought to do that.

Or maybe they'd just laugh. The phone rang inside the house. It went on ringing.

Back in my bedroom, I lay belly down on my bed, with a chess set. One my Auntie bought me when she came to visit from Sydney, where you press the piece you're about to move into its spot on the board and press it again on the spot it moves to. Then the computer beneath the black and white squares lights up on two sides of the board in red lights to tell me which piece to move for it, and where to. I could be the black or white pieces, and I used to always be white, and now I'm always black. Today I go white. Playing chess was the quiet thing to do when the baby was napping. But I can play even when it's noisy. Even if the baby is crying. Even if my mum is angry at the things she is cooking for burning or taking so long. The sounds of her moving around like that in the kitchen make me feel things are normal.

Soon I'll have to go in there to make my own breakfast if they don't get up. I've done it before. I can make scrambled eggs. If there's any shell in the bowl with the yellow and clear part of the egg I'll take it out with my pinkie. Someone told me once that the chickens come from that yellow part. I don't know why they come out all white then, like the shell outside. I suppose people are all red on the inside, and we come from a red spot like that in a mother. It's like the secret colour for a chicken is yellow, and for a person it is red, like the lights on the side of the chess board. The black and white spaces we move over, from here to there, are like secret colours below the green grass and grey concrete. And if I'm white now, maybe I'm black inside. Maybe the secret of the stars is heaven. The secret of my baby sister is my mother. There are probably secrets in things like trees as well. If they eat the sunlight, as the teachers say, then maybe it's a sun inside them. I play chess for hours sometimes. I can almost beat level three. I wonder what happens if I beat level six. That would be the same as reaching two minutes of holding my breath. When I started playing this chess set I didn't know the way all the pieces moved. I thought the pawns could move like checkers until the computer started beeping, angry red lights flashing. Now I understand the pieces better, and what they can do together, but I didn't know that at the start. I don't know what I'll know at level six, or if I hold my breath for two minutes, but it would be different from now, and maybe then I'll understand the secrets.

I went out to water the grass. It's what my dad did. He enjoyed waving the hose around the lawn and we have a lot of grass. In the back yard we also have trees. Lemon trees and a plum tree, but I'm not sure if it's plums it is supposed to grow because that one never gave any fruit in all the years he has watered it. And sometimes the watering would go on for a whole episode of *The Simpsons*. He said he could think outside. I didn't understand why he couldn't think in the house like everybody else. But I went out there to see what he was talking about. I unrolled the hose from its special wheel. I turned it on and watched the thing fly around like a snake gone berserk. It almost wet me but I knew how to grab the hose and bend it over so it could only dribble. The reason it did that, go berserk, is because I had stepped on the orange and grey swively thing at the top of it.

I'd broken a lot of things around the house. It never made sense to me, though. It seemed stupid to make glass that could be broken by a volley ball. When my dad got angry at me for the orange swively thing I told him they should make those things out of something tougher. Was I supposed to watch where I put every step all the time? My dad smiled when I said those things. I knew when I was being smart, though not why it was smart.

Maybe it was just him thinking it, repeating it like it was, "No, I suppose you can't watch where you put down every foot." And then because he was my dad, "But I tell you what, you break another one of these things, I might take it out of your pocket money. I think that's fair, hey? If I walked into your room, and stepped on your computer chessboard, you'd expect me to buy you a new one, hey?" He put 'hey' on the end of his sentences a lot. I didn't hear anyone else doing that but it was his way of asking me questions gently. I asked him about something I heard my mother say on the phone, about our baby being an accident, and my father said there were no accidents. Things happened for a reason. There were secrets about why, but accidents just had explanations we couldn't see.

When I went out to water the grass for him I was thinking about those kinds of things. About a world that had no accidents. And everything having a reason. I thought about the grass and how it always seemed to grow as long as you cut it with the lawnmower every month and watered it every day. I thought that if I watered it every day for the rest of my life it would always be green like this. Grass didn't go grey, or bald, and if you kept watering it, it never died. And I wished I could ask my dad if that was true. Because if I had children, and it all went on like that for hundreds of years, and we never forgot to water the grass, would it keep growing, and stay green forever? I thought about coming out here every day and doing that. I knew I wasn't good with promises so I didn't make one. I watered the lemon trees and the other one as well. Whatever kind of tree it was, hey?

Yesterday the house was filled with shouting and screaming. Arguments about me and my sister and whose fault it was that she was sick so often and why I wasn't getting good enough grades in school and was moping around the house all day instead of being normal and playing with other boys in the neighbourhood. Their voices felt like they were ripping up the air and shreds of it rained down into every corner of our house, amid the sound of baby teething, and who knew what her problem was anyway. Just unhappy about being dragged into this world. Maybe everything hurts out here. And I lay next to my bed, put my face down to the carpet, and listened. To my parents more than anything. Just wanting them to finish. Even when they did stop, they started up again, like they hated each other and wanted it to hurt and wanted it to last forever; wanted it to bleed without cutting through the skin first. That's what it felt like just listening to it—getting sliced up inside but I couldn't show where it got through on my face or my chest. And then later, there's my mother calling to me, with a tremor in her voice, which is a kind of laughter I suppose, as my father giggle-grapples with her limbs, trying to kiss her, and me being called in to stop them falling in love again. I think it's hard to let go of hate and anger and to forget how much they both sometimes hated our family.

Today the house is filled with something else. I lie down on the carpet, with the side of my face in the threads of it. It's hard to keep my eyes closed. My eyes want to look at whatever they can find. The pieces of a jigsaw puzzle I never put together because it had too much blue sky and grass in it, pushed in a pile under my bed, and the dust along the skirting board, thick on the part that was under my bed. My ears find the silence in the carpet but I can feel my blood getting hot in my face. Boiling up all my thoughts as well, so I can't tell what I'm thinking, but wish that I wasn't. I wish that there was a pause on thinking, but it never stops for a second.

It's too cold for the pool outside, but I go out and I take off my clothes, even my underpants, and go down into the shivering water, holding my breath, with a hand on the ladder in the deep end. I try to count the seconds but I lose track. I want to cross over two minutes. I imagine I'm a jigsaw puzzle. I scatter in a drift across the bottom of the pool, and if I'm blue like the water, like the egg is yellow underneath the white, then no-one will ever be able to put me together again, not with all their horses and all their men. I know it doesn't make sense. But it's hard to make sense if you're like a tree that never makes any fruit. You spend your whole life wondering about lemons or plums or something else. Something strange that tastes like chlorine. Good to eat only for mermaids.

They will ask me what I did. Why a whole day went by, and how a whole day passed like this, and I will not be able to say that their lips were blue and their faces had turned the colour of wet concrete and that there was a bubble of blood on the surface of it. I won't be able to say that if I put my finger through it, to break it open, I would have smeared it into a smudge of red and heard the murmurs of them down below the hardening surface. They will ask how and why but I will not be able to explain about voice smudges popping in bubbles through my brain.

The sun was getting through at the edges of those wooden Venetian blinds my father wanted to buy for the whole house but could only afford to put them in his study. He made my mother say a thousand times over that it gave the house a pirate face, and she meant that it was like a patch over one eye. "We'll get a red parrot one day to sit on the roof. Dress the kids in black scarves around their heads." He was going to do the whole house, he said, but the baby came so early she could have fit in my school bag with all my school stuff easy, and then mum was so sick at the hospital that she couldn't work anymore because she couldn't stop crying some days. She spent a lot of time yelling and hitting me and then sitting on the couch for hours with the TV and stereo off, and "Listening to the house creaking," she said.

I'm sitting in the armchair my father sits in when he's reading. There are books everywhere, and I think he's read most of them. Lots have bookmarks in them, so maybe he got a certain way through those before stopping. I don't come in here all that often because it's boring in here with no TV, and not even music. There are newspapers and books, paper and pens, and a computer that doesn't seem to be able to do anything. All it's good for is dad and his writing. I picked out some of the books. He's not the kind of person to write something in them anywhere, but that would be good. To see what he was thinking when some guy in one of them says he knew *every raindrop by its name*. Did he think that's smart like he thought I am sometimes, or is it as stupid as it sounds to me? You can't be sure. Can't be sure of anything. Even one plus one, which works when it's something as simple as coins, but not if it's something like cats, hey? Two cats in a room don't feel like two cats in a room. It just feels like cats, doing what they do, sleeping most of the time, or making their way on the edges of furniture, from the desk to the chair, to the window ledge, to the bookshelves, as though the floor was too boring for them, and two has got nothing to do with anything. If one of the cats leaves the room, is it two minus one? One cat in the room. And what about if that cat leaves the room? Is the sum then, zero, no cats in the room? Because that's not really true. There's stuff like cat hair, and where the cat clawed the side of the couch and got in trouble but still did it anyway. I think I was thinking about cats because we had one before baby came along. Dad said the cat died and didn't go to heaven because there was no such thing as heaven. But where does God live then? He said there was a secret about God, and no-one knows it yet. Our cat was part of the secret now. I don't know what he was talking about. I just don't think one minus one means zero, unless it's something like coins you want to talk about. I'm sitting in his armchair, and I can smell him. I look at the books with bookmarks in them and want to pull them out but I don't. I just sit there doing nothing. Unless you call doing maths with cats something.

A knock on the back door, and my name called out. I close all the doors. Through the large glass sliding door and patio windows Peter can see me closing my parents' bedroom door. Me and Pete walk to school together every day. He's never late. I don't know how he does it, because it's not his parents. Both of them wake up before six to go somewhere far away for work. He's only late to school because of me. He sees that I'm in my pyjamas and his face falls open a millimetre or two, because he can't believe it even if he isn't surprised.

"Come on, fuck you, Coultas." We'd begun swearing all the time. And using our surnames instead of our other ones. "Come on man, fuck."

I slide open the door. He walks in and goes for the coffee. He's only twelve, but he drinks a lot of coffee. Maybe that's why he didn't have trouble in the mornings, but I didn't think it was that. As he waits for the kettle, with his back to me, he yawns. Loudly. Every time it shakes me up. I don't know why. It's really some kind of roar.

"I'm not fucking coming today, Hately. You still asleep or what?"

"Why?" He turns around. "You fucken look all right." The kettle pops and he pours it over his coffee and sugar. Stirs it. Adds heaps of milk. It still looks pretty dark though.

"Something's happened," I say.

"No shit." He takes a loud slurp. "What about Belcher's maths test?"

He wasn't smart in any remarkable way but he always tried harder than anyone else. It usually worked for him. I thought of myself as the one with natural abilities, and flair, but maybe that's what all lazy people convince themselves of. If we put in the effort it would be easier for us than those who work at it, and we could do anything… meanwhile doing nothing. Belcher hated me, and there was no way I was going to pass this year's maths. Next year I was going to be able to drop maths altogether. I couldn't believe it. Kids allowed not to worry about maths. We have computers and calculators to do that kind of thing. But didn't they spend years convincing us maths was vital, like the secret of the world was in a logarithm, whatever that was anyway. They should make up their minds, hey?

"Why don't you hang around. We can play the…"

He snaps, "Did you hear what I said?" Again that yawn rattles my ribs. He finishes with his mug of coffee and leaves it, still half full and steaming, on the bench. Walks for the door. "You're fucken mental, Coultas." And leaves.

He's the same every morning. I don't know why he keeps coming around if he's that pissed off with me jerking him around.

I don't actually think we're friends even though we play cricket or kick-to-kick out on our street. We call each other friends because we live close to each other and we're the same age and it's better to do stuff like walking to school or playing sport with someone. He might like me a bit but I'm pretty sure he hates me as well.

Kids that are your friends one day at school seem to suddenly go off you. I go off people as well, but more often it's because they're doing it to me and I don't want them to know it. We're all pretending we don't care about things like who likes us and who doesn't, so we don't look as if we're weak. But I didn't choose to be like this, and none of us can help it, so we might as well be honest. But we aren't. The best thing to do is pretend that nothing hurts.

I wash out his mug. There's another mug there that I left from last night but didn't use. I wash that as well for no good reason. I wait and wonder what I should do, now that I'm not going to school. I keep getting some kind of static in my head. I want to stop thinking. That should be possible. I wish it was.

I walk around our home hearing their voices, on the verge of making out words. It's a tone of voice, a sound words make in her throat, in the empty air around me that lets me know it's my mother. In my father's throat. I can hear all of us, as though the sound of our family is coming out of the walls. Almost hear us all alive. Soon the anonymous voices, and the loud clomping around, making my home anonymous in their what-needed-to-be-done-now stamping, will kill these sounds. I can see the echoes from the corners of my eyes, in the reflections of the pictures and paintings we have hanging on the walls. I glimpse the movement of my father's walk, which has a careful shuffle in it that barely anyone would notice. The terrible sickness of his body that kept him hospitalised from his teen years to his twenties. Wasting those years that should have been something else. I walk around thinking I can feel and see and smell echoes.

At night I pull out some fish fingers from the fridge and bake them in the grill. I cut a lemon as well and squeeze it over them. I don't have bread but maybe fish fingers don't really need bread. I reckon they're best the way dad makes them, and not mum, who prefers to give them to me on rice, with vegies. My dad says there's nothing like that soft white texture wrapped around crusty food. I watch television, but there's something wrong with my head because I can't understand anything. People run around doing things that don't connect with anything else. They say things like puppets, like the Punch and Judy pantomime I saw last year at school, where it was all screeching wah-wah-wah, whack, and more screeching, wah-wah-wah, whack. Doesn't matter which channel I switch to. Even my favourite recorded shows don't work anymore. *Ferris Bueller's Day Off* doesn't make sense either, and it scares me how watching something I've seen fifty times before, where I know whole parts off by heart have broken into pieces that don't fit. So I wander away from the television.

There are clothes on the Hills Hoist that my mother left from the day before. She should have asked me to bring them in hours ago, because it's dark now. I take out the washing basket and stand under all our clothes. I wind it down so I can reach the pegs. The clothes are dry, even stiff, because it might have rained a little during the previous night. I take off the pegs and put the clothes into the basket. My body is starting not to work anymore either. I keep lifting my arms. Making my fingers work. Pulling everything off. I put all the pegs in the special peg basket they are meant to go into. I pick up the washing basket but I can't walk. The house has all its lights on, but it doesn't make sense like *Ferris Bueller's* doesn't make sense.

My parents haven't gotten out of bed all day. My sister hasn't cried once and she cries all the time. I know what it means but I don't want to think. It should be possible to stop but no matter how hard I try, I can't. When you hold your breath for long enough the world gets dark and quiet and I wanted to move into that place as though it was a quiet cave but you can't trick the body. It forces you to breathe again.

I don't walk towards the house because of the problem with my legs and my arms and my body and my head. I move to the side of the pool wanting to walk right across it. But I stop. Drop the basket into the water. All our clothes move across the water instead of me. They float with the lights in the side of the pool reaching up and making me feel so dizzy I want to go inside there to feel the light turn me blue. I see the floating clothes moving in the water. And their naked blue bodies with blue lips drift in the blue water below and disappear into more blue. I want to go into the water with them and believe in the mermaid's secret. If she had kissed me that day maybe I would know how to live without air.

But I don't go into the water. I don't want to drown again. I'm afraid that it's just lungfuls of heavy water, like it was lungfuls of poison air, and there's just a million times a million blades of grass all living and dying by themselves. They seem green but blue is the secret colour and it doesn't matter what you do, the grass is always dying.

I wander out into the street and walk around. I want it to rain so that I can see if each raindrop knows my name like that man in my dad's book said. I walk from one street light to another. They each seem to greet me and to have been waiting for me to visit. So I stop and listen to the electrical hum you have to be very quiet to hear. Rain would make it easier to listen to their voices hissing and whispering. I walk from one street light to another, after a while coming back around to where we used to live. A house with one eye patched like a pirate.

A neighbour's house has all their lights on. A Christmas tree in the window even though Christmas was finished more than a month ago. Mr. Steed lives in there. He's the neighbour that told me there were men who could hold their breath for ten minutes.

I knock on the door. I wait and hear footsteps. Voices inside joke and complain, are told to stop it, and then I hear, "The Coultas kid." Because the Steeds can see me from their lounge room window. The voices will turn into questions and answers. A million of them. I won't know what to say because they'll be hard to tell apart like the jigsaw puzzle beneath my bed that I couldn't put together because it had too much of a blue sky and long fields of green grass.

I wanted to make a hot chocolate and I changed my mind. I got distracted by my mother screaming at my father about going to look after my baby sister who was crying. There was so much noise and the air was hissing with their anger I felt like I was suffocating and I forgot to light the gas so that it would turn into a fire. All I wanted to do was warm the milk, but I forgot and got distracted. It's a very easy thing to do. But I don't know how I'll explain. Why their bedroom door was open and mine was closed.

My father told me there were no accidents. That there was a reason for everything.

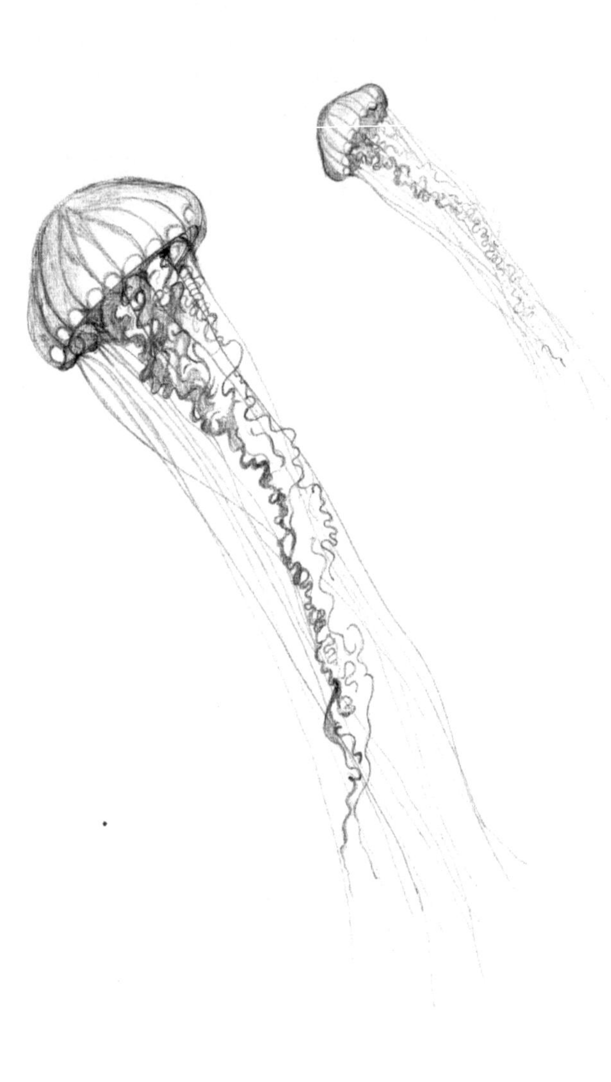

Serpentine Red

There was a red light, blinking, with long lazy moments in between, in the corner of my eye. Day and night, a little red light, flashing.

It was such a tiny thing I thought I was imagining it. Too many hours in front of a computer screen; exhaustion. I used to stare at the sun when I was a child, and though I'd heard this can cause blindness, I didn't think it was the reason for that tiny light at the edge of my vision, ceaselessly pulsing.

Sleep became impossible. With heavy doses of sleeping pills, I found unconsciousness only briefly. It was as disturbing during the daytime, when there was a light blue sky above, almost white at its edges. Or on a tram with commuters wearing their flat browns, greys and blacks. In the office with its off-white walls. The red flashing didn't stop. Wouldn't stop flashing for a moment.

I was fired from my job. They didn't buy the story about a little red light in my eye. My girlfriend had been planning to move in with me. She'd even given up her lease, but she changed her mind, and cried every time she saw me. Then — she wouldn't answer my calls.

I went to a doctor and asked him to remove my left eye. The doctor wanted to lock me up for suggesting I take out the faulty organ. I avoided getting put away by saying, with firebreathing conviction, that I was a journalist researching the medical establishment's widespread mishandling of the mentally ill. I said that of course there was nothing wrong with my eye. Of course I didn't want to get it pulled out of its socket.

A few days later I took more painkillers than recommended. I washed them down with so much vodka that I could barely get a grip of the slim cheese knife on the basin's edge. The red light was blinking so persistently and brightly by that point I didn't really hesitate.

I held the upper lid and lower lid parted with thumb and forefinger as I pushed the knife deep inside the white of that left eye and popped it out. It hung from the optic nerve. Weeks without sleep and relentless distress had created the hysteria leading to this point. I didn't have the sense though to understand the bulb of the eye came with a thick attachment to the brain. I was on the verge of being paralytic but waking up on the bathroom floor a few hours later, with my left eye dangling from the optic nerve, was a thought more horrifying that what had to happen next. The bathroom scissors used for trimming weren't sharp. I was ready to either plunge them into my throat or cut loose that left eye — that even now was flashing, ceaselessly pulsing red.

Those small silver scissors in my drunken fingers, slippery with the blood that I'd already shed, cut away at the nerve. The pain was obliterating and I was writhing and moaning on the butcher's floor of my bathroom but the eye came loose.

There was no more flashing red light and the relief of that darkness, that stillness, was a liquid ecstasy only a creature of the deepest ocean would understand after having been dragged by a metal hook for days. I wanted to drift deeper and let the currents of alcohol and drugs drown me in perfect darkness. I crawled to bed with my eyes closed and slept over twenty-four hours. I got up and had a big plate of eggs and bacon with another dose of painkillers. Had a litre of orange juice and went back to bed and slept for another twelve.

I had a multitude of dreams but I dreamed so many things I forgot what was history, what was memory, what was imagination and what creative impulse generated the goldfish and the whale from the same oceanic secret. I'd been out walking seabeds as far as the South China Sea and to the Pearl River Delta. Deep within the fragrant harbour of Hong Kong, a Dragon Princess came close and whispered into my mouth that the seed of our history is passed with a kiss.

The eyeball was in the bathroom sink when I felt ready for the world again. I checked for the damage done within the socket but didn't find the hacked nerve endings I was expecting. That's not what I saw inside that left socket in the mirror. It was something serpentine and red in a black oil behind a thick membrane.

I moved closer to the mirror. I wasn't afraid that I was losing my mind. I'd never been clearer in my thoughts. There was no more pain and I was calm. Rock-solid after the long sleep. No matter how long I stood with my face to the mirror I couldn't work out what was moving around behind the empty socket.

I put on sunglasses and went out for air. I strolled about and found my way down to a park by St Kilda beach. I sat in a gazebo and listened to the noises people made walking around the park; kicking their footballs around; walking their dogs; walking each other, hand in hand. When the sun went down I took my sunglasses off.

What a blessing everything on the planet seemed to me in that moment. Every little thing in it, tied into everything else.

The way grass needed the sun and wind to grow and propagate. Creatures that fed and grew from that green life, and men that lived from the flesh of those creatures. In the spreading red light of the sunset I could see that human bodies were no different — that life needed to feed and grow from our blood as well. Everything connected, and leading on to culminations we rarely saw.

I walked along St Kilda pier and thousands of jellyfish swam past the wooden pylons holding me aloft. Within their soft heads was the large glowing knot of their minds. I'd never seen jellyfish glowing like that before. I stopped to watch them drift. They were unable to swim like other fish. They used the tides and currents to move. They were too close to shore now and tomorrow the beaches would be littered with their fragile bodies.

I ambled over the long pier until I reached the cluster of rocks that was a home to penguins and slid down off the path to the water's edge. It was so dark below my feet that it looked like the oil-like substance in my head.

I moved closer to the water. It was a black mirror that swallowed every reflection. I felt my body becoming heavy. I sat down and when my limbs went rigid, I could do nothing but lean over the massive boulder beneath me. My arms gripped the rock with a rigour I couldn't control. It got worse and I couldn't move. And then I couldn't swallow. Or blink. My lungs were the only parts of me unaffected. I breathed across the oily membrane of black water in slow breaths.

This body was a cocoon for me long before I realised there was another life waiting to emerge from the husk. It only became clear in the final moments of this transition. I slipped through the socket of the skull like a monstrous octopus that can compress its vast bulk and squeeze through the diameter of a red apple.

What the Dragon Princess said is true, (though when I met her on a layover in Hong Kong she was a pretty Chinese photographer strolling through my hotel lobby) the seed of our serpentine lives is passed through our mouths. We find other ways to emerge from our skins.

Forgotten Things

Dear Gail,

They tell me I'll be getting out in a few days. I don't want you to be afraid. I've been afraid. You don't tell it from looking at me in the mirror. I can't see it myself but it's fucking in there. Sometimes it feels like gasoline lit up. It feels like dying so much sometimes you want it to just come on and burn you the hell up already. It keeps the hellfire going and that's what the priest means by how it never stops. Eternal damnation and all that shit but I get up in the mornings and I look in the mirror and it's not there. Not in the mirror. I just see a skull wrapped in hair and skin. My teeth are the exposed bones. I suppose the skull belongs to me. Who else would want it? I'm missing two teeth in my top jaw now and one in the bottom. I lost a canine in a fight. Lucky I didn't lose the two front ones. You still wouldn't want to see me smile I reckon. Without one of the front ones you look stupid. Like ha-ha stupid. But you wouldn't like the look of me these days. Believe me. Those fucken eyes don't seem familiar even to me. I don't see that fear. That's not what I hope for you. You should believe me. Haven't I kept my mouth shut this long? For eight fucking years. So why would you be worried now? It makes me think of that song about how you need to be a worried man to sing a worried song. So if I talk about fear it's not because I want to put it into you. I just want you to know it's there. That I've put it into many men in here with me, but I'm not going to put it into you. I wonder though how much you already own for yourself. I know you've got new children now. But I remember the first one. I remember you busting to go to the toilet and holding onto your piss because we had to go in and find out how old the thing inside you was. The guy called it a jellybean. He told me to listen to the heart beat. And I saw that little thing flashing like it's meant to be the heart. But twice as quick as mine or yours. Like it's running but only 'cause it was growing. Growing quicker than any kind of running. Double her size every few weeks. I remember looking into that screen like I was seeing something from another planet. Somewhere like Venus. He said seven weeks. Imagine being seven weeks old and then imagine me in here for the eight years of manslaughter. I reckon I'd be on another planet on that screen as well. Somewhere like the Sun. But black. Like it was swallowed by something ugly. And them saying I was lucky for only eight years. As though my life hasn't already been fucken wasted. Opposite direction for me than a baby. I'm shrinking. Like one of those old kinds of Asprin. The tablet in the water. Dissolving. The Jellybean was that small as well. That's how old it was then when we saw its heart and heard it beating. Somewhere in you Gail. Seven weeks and racing. It was also somewhere inside me. Me and the fear. That's what I've had growing. Double and double again. Growing like it's running. You remember when it was like that. When you could barely think, there was so much fire right through you. So they say they're going to let me out now. Only a few more days of the eight years left but I haven't changed for the better. None of us do. The kind of life they give us in here there's only one way you come out the iron gates. Worse. Just worse in every fucking way. You might think I'm looking forward to it. But I'm not. The fear turns into something else out there. It changes into something that cuts instead of burns. There's only one way for it to go then. To stop it from cutting me it's got to cut someone else. You understand, don't you? Because I might've put the knife in but you kissed the spot first. I know I've got be careful in a letter not to talk about that kind of thing. I've kept me mouth shut though and you should believe me when I tell you. It's not because of any of this that I'm writing you. It's a question I want to ask. Does she know she's mine? That she's something that came from me? That I saw her heart beating double fast like that? Saw it flashing like it was a signal through the white clouds of Venus, saying to me, "You Belong To Me And I Belong To You." That's all I want to know. Whether you lied or you told the truth.

Yours sincerely

Oliver
December 8

Dear Gail,

I'm rattling along from Epping to Frankston. I go from Williamstown to Belgrave. I cross bridges and pass schools and churches and hospitals and graveyards and parks and I see Port Phillip Bay and the Yarra and other rivers like the Maribyrnong. I get on trains to see everything passing along as though time didn't matter. As though people didn't matter. Outside the windows of the train it's houses and what happens inside doesn't really matter too much. The houses are always there. It doesn't matter who comes and goes. All day long I see people getting on and getting off the trains. Women with babies in their stomachs like they'd swallowed stones, or the babies are shoved in their prams like sacks. There's boys and girls in school clothes talking like the world was invented for them. People reading the paper or books and seeing none of what's right here in front of them. If they see me, it's nothing but fear. It's all about the past and the future no matter how hard I try to stay here in the now. None of these people want to stay here either. The mother wants her child to just shut up from crying and imagines it getting bigger and finding her happily-ever-after. What if the baby never grows up at all? What would she think about that? How long would she hold onto that baby? How many years? What if the book of that man over there never changes its pages, and he reads the same page a hundred times? Then a thousand times? There's that old woman wearing too much cheap jewellery that makes me think of your mother and how she was never going to do anything but get older and older. Shrink into her crumpled old skin that looked like an old coat someone forgot on a train station. Never die and just get older and older. These kids in uniforms. They're the only happy ones. The train moves quickly and they tumble out with their heavy bags laughing like I don't exist and you don't exist and none of what's in the houses matter. I pass your station as well and I know you still live in your mother's house in Spotswood. The West Gate Bridge climbs up high at Spotswood station. It's a beautiful place in the ugly of it all and I'd like to see you again. One more time. There's something I need to do first. If I bring something it won't be bread and milk on my way home like I used to do. It'll be stones to fill your stomach with. A needle to sew you up and then we'll climb the bridge again. Because that's what you did to me, Gail. You gave me a belly full of stones, and if the water below was the place we killed your mother, then you pushed me in along with her.

Your mother didn't deserve what we did. Doesn't matter how she'd turned into such an old coat of skin forgetting everyone that had worn her out. I know I deserved what I got. Which is why I'm staying away and keeping my stones to myself for now. But I'm wondering how come you received nothing of what you deserved? I ride along the trains from Alamein to Melton. I'm riding now from Werribee to Hurstbridge. Passing along from Eaglemont to Heidelberg. It's green around here but it's getting dark now and everyone is beginning to light up their houses. I think about my Emily and I know I can't stay away forever. For days now I've been getting off at Spotswood. I stand beneath the bridge and I know you are somewhere close. I watch people get off the train. They move out into the streets and disappear into the houses. Some of them towards you and the house we lived in together. I get back on the train and take it all the way out to Lilydale.

Yours truly

Oliver Irvine
January 28

Dear Gail,

I want to thank you for the picture of Emily you put in with your last letter to me. Too many years have gone by since then but I'm grateful for that anyway. She looks like a bright little girl. Like she has enough light in her for both of us. But if I think about what I could bring her now I know I'd just swallow her into that black sun inside me. And I don't want anyone else with me here. Except you. We could close our eyes together one last time, the way we used to do when the house was dark and quiet at night. I don't know if it's even fair to blame you for your mother because it wasn't you that made her forget everything or put her in that sack of confusion and it wasn't you that gave her diabetes on top of the Alzheimer's. Then there's the sugar and the wrong pills we gave her instead of her medicine. You might have told me to do it but I done it, didn't I? I put too much on you I know. Sometimes it seems it wasn't anyone's fault. We lose the light we had when we were the age Emily is now. It gets darker so much quicker than we can get ready for. Then we just try to make our way to wherever we can see a bit of light. In those early days below the West Gate there was light in that house with you, and I think we were stupid and we were cruel. But not all the time, and the light was real, and it doesn't matter about anything else. That was real and you can call it love. It hasn't been easy for me Gail. I know it's been hard on you as well. But with me there's just wanting to die and wanting to murder and for a long time I didn't see anything else. So it was back and forth from Pakenham to Sydenham, Sandringham to Upfield. Trying to find something else and knowing I wasn't going to be able to do it. I knew I'd be getting off at Spotswood again. I got off the train and I never wanted to get back on. I walked down the streets to your place. I came to the front gate. It was almost off its hinges because there was no one around to fix it. There was a little bike there on the grass. It had training wheels on it. The thought came to me that I wasn't a beast anymore like I used to have to be inside. Inside the walls and gates and inside myself as well. I don't know what would've happened without that bike being there on the path and not wanting to step over it or throw it aside. Such a little thing with pink plastic pedals that looked as though they were made of candy. But who am I to decide what should have happened with your mother? It wasn't my place and it wasn't yours. Or maybe it was yours because a daughter eats her mother's pain every day when they live in the same house. I don't understand it all but I knew it wasn't mine to say to Emily, here I am to take your mother from you because she threw me away into the darkness and didn't come to visit and did everything she could to forget me. The darkness was there before you as well, Gail. And I've always been stupid. Stupid to think you brought me light when you were lost in the darkness as well. I didn't have anything to do with my days these past few months but rock side to side along the train tracks. Going everywhere they could take me around Melbourne. I was trying to think for the first time in my stupid life. Not just go over things again and again but to see if I could understand how it happened that I was on the train watching all these people going from here to there as though it all belonged to them. How none of it belonged to me. Not the seat I was sitting on or even the clothes I've been wearing. Barely even my own body anymore because wasn't I ready to just chuck it off a bridge like a sack of stones? For months I've been looking into people's backyards all over Melbourne. There were clotheslines with shirts and underwear and bath towels. There were dogs barking and a few chicken coops. There were old rusting cars surrounded by tall grass and all kinds of forgotten things. People were mowing lawns or standing there just talking with someone. Or they were by themselves having a smoke looking at the train I was on, going by. All those backyards you could see from the trains. Late at night, I'd be in the carriage by myself, and it was like all the trains were empty as well. I'd think about you and how Emily looked at seven weeks and those pictures of her on Venus. That one picture you sent to me in prison. It got me through the eight years and that's the only thing I'll keep of her. And now there's nothing in Melbourne that belongs to me anymore. So

 The Rattler & other stories

there's nothing to keep me. If the train's empty with me on it then that's a good thing. It means all I need to do is throw the sack of stones onto a seat and let the train go somewhere else. There's winter coming, and in Melbourne there's the cold and dark, which goes on for such a long time. Someone inside told me that it never gets cold up north. It just gets wet. That there's light from five to eight. Even in the dead of winter.

Oliver Irvine
May 2011

Some Kind of Blues

My mother and father spoke Serbian. When they laughed there was a resonance of that language in the sound they made. They yelled in it when they argued. The television used a different language but we spoke in Serbian during the commercials. We ate our meals with it. My mother tore strips of flesh off us with it. In the evenings, as we got ready to go to bed, Serbian was a whispered language invoking gentle dreams. It sometimes felt like a secret language devised for our house and family alone. I went to school and spoke English and crossed the border every afternoon at about three-thirty without noticing.

One day, I walked past a woman sitting in her car, outside a milk-bar on the corner of our street. She was yelling out the open window, *you fucking, fucking, dumb, fucking, fucking, stupid, fucken, fucken, fucken...* Her child couldn't find what she needed from the store, and he was going to have to go back in there and get it. No excuses. It was salt, or it was flour. There was no chance the milk-bar didn't have it. It seemed easier for her to shout obscenities at him than to get out and find it herself. The boy was staring wide-eyed at his mother, stunned by that spitting fury, until a girl on roller-skates came hurtling around the corner of the milk bar and almost ran him over. The boy looked around and saw there were children staring at him and his angry mother. He lowered his head and went back into the store.

I must have been six or seven, and appalled at the language, because I told my mother (who said the *f-word* if she needed to refer to the expression at all) what had happened. I realised that even though she didn't swear in English, she said all that and worse—bizarre combinations of the Serbian *f-word* equivalent and the sun, and God, mothers and dogs. I had not understood, until that moment, that they were swear words in the same way that the word *fuck* was a swear word in English. My mother had got a job in the civil service and learned how to speak English fluently. It became her language at home with us more and more, but it would always be a polite language, softly spoken, with nothing closer to passion for it than the delicate reference to the *f-word*.

It didn't mean anything. And it didn't need to. But then… it does. You can't help it. You don't decide. It's some kind of mathematics working itself out in the bones for cave men who haven't yet worked out the symbols for + and − or =, contemplating the fractions within themselves and the fractals of their future. It's some kind of calculation that results in words as much as blood, in life and history, and then somehow still means nothing.

Walking to school, and looking at a new coin. It wasn't that shiny, but it said 1980 on it, and that was the current year. Before that I'd assumed everything in the world was already within it before I came along. We had just begun building a house on Power Street, so things were happening as I walked the footpath to school that had never happened before. The world was built, complete, but things were incomplete as well, and under construction. And, I would discover, there was also demolition.

That year, on my birthday, Tito died. That could have meant a pet dog, or some neighbour, or who knew? But my

THE RATTLER & OTHER STORIES

mother cried. It was as real as someone on a television show dying (and a show I'd never seen at that), but my mother crying made it feel like it was worth being sad about. I don't know if I got any presents that year, but I remember her saying that perhaps she shouldn't give me any, and maybe it was some kind of curse. I was just starting primary school and important people who should live forever were leaving the planet. Images on the television showed us people mourning Tito. Processions and flag-draped coffins, though maybe that imagined footage comes courtesy of JFK. And others, in the streets celebrating as if it was New Year's. First time I saw a burning effigy—and that didn't come from film stock. Across the ocean somewhere, it meant something. Over here it couldn't have meant less. Who was Tito? No-one really cares anymore.

But I find myself curious, asking irrelevant questions and finding pointless answers. I imagine that boy in the first grade walking to school with a new coin in his pocket, but I know there are other clothes on the hangers at home, pockets filled with the coins of the Romans and the Ottomans, and ones with the profile of Tito embossed on every one. A figure in coins I'd never seen, never used, whose value could never be determined, and never be exchanged or converted.

Tito was Yugoslavia. The heads when you tossed a coin. Spinning in the air so long that no-one was sure how he even came by the name. A Croatian that the Serbians loved and that the Croatians hated. A dictator who ruled with less violence than most of the presidents the Americans have produced in their democratic history. Who took a people descended from one tongue and bloodline, but torn up amongst the hungry powers of Empires that were always circling, and gave them a generation of unity and peace. Who died, and then—as if in the same funeral procession—a nation followed into death. And of course, generalisations like these say nothing about the moods of the people he governed who went about their daily lives ruled by their own passions of heart and spleen; their own aspirations and fears.

There are those who will say it was inevitable, that the bloodshed to come was predictable, from what was known of these Southern Slavs, (which has always been almost nothing). There were many who died in the making of unity. There were many more who loved it dearly, and more still, who knew the wars were not inevitable.

Spain had been an Islamic nation until the Christians killed all its Muslims. England a Catholic nation until its Protestants converted and killed all who stood in the way of Protestant unity. Inevitable or predictable, Yugoslavia was a nation of Catholic and Orthodox Christians, Muslims and Jews, who all wanted to live freely amongst each other, sharing a past and a future. But they lived with the threat of sabotage. Sabotage executed by radicals who know that the firing of guns is the best way to silence the reasonable and peaceable.

So, for the curious child, who was Tito? Not a hero. He was the beatific face put into a frame and stuck onto walls in homes, and his smile had some kind of answer to that threat of sabotage.

I walked to school with new coins and old, reading their dates, the word Commonwealth on all of them. Queen Elizabeth on every one, and I thought she looked pretty. She was someone else far across the waters. If she'd died, all of those coins would have been changed. Tito's death meant something in my house, and I didn't know what. I didn't really care all that much. Same as singing the national anthem, looking up at the blue flag with its stars, and the British flag stitched into the corner didn't mean much.

A Union Jack heritage, or flags less prominently incorporated into our identity, are clues to something altogether more enigmatic. Because that scrap of cloth in the corner of our flag doesn't mean anything, and then it does. We don't get to choose. The difference between childhood and everything that comes after is simple arithmetic. What we can't calculate goes into the ever after beyond the equal sign. Everything that happened before is a different kind of sum. A mathematics of bones within a theory of soul. A place we've all been but can never know.

The question was—What are you? Despite clearly being raised in the same country, with Victorian-only footy and Lily, Marsh and Chappell cricket, Hawke and Labor, the boxing kangaroo and *Australia II, Flame Trees* every morning before school for weeks, and Molly Meldrum's *Count Down* on Sundays, singing the new anthem of Men at Work's *Down Under*, wearing the same clothes and speaking the same accented English, still that was the question. Or it was, What nationality are you? which, if it's looked at like that, would make you assume that there was some drastic difference between me and the general population. But kids asked each other that question all the time, and that was the way to ask, despite the differences often being invisible.

What are you? What's your nationality? There wasn't an insult to it because it didn't seem a deviation from something fixed. Rather, a definite quality, in contrast to an abstract principle. If someone was Australian, with no recourse to answering what they were, it meant Anglo-Saxon. In this context Australian meant nothing. To be Un-Australian, a little like a mind-bending Zen Koan. But being something called Serbian, or Yugoslav as it was when Bob Hawke seemed to me the father of my country, was equally mystifying. If I was from another continent, outside of Europe, it would have been easier to identify an array of cultural divergences. But there wasn't much, other than the language at home, to make me feel different. There was a variation on Christianity. That we crossed ourselves in a different way, was all

I knew for certain about being an Orthodox Christian. Other Europeans like the Greeks had different cuisine, but we mostly ate the food I saw advertised on television.

Children define themselves within different contexts, and while we work out how we fit or how we don't, television can be a perspective on the broader world beyond our immediate suburban realities. Watching *Australia II* win the America's Cup wasn't a news item on a broadcast. It was a defining moment for me as to what Australia was and what it could be. Watching Denis Lilly race up to a cricket crease with the crowd chanting his name (red stains down his white pants resembling smears of blood), gave me a sense of the heroic for the first time in my life. I was a child in a suburban lounge-room watching television when the land of my ancestors erupted into the most horrific explosion of violence in the modern era.

Horror films usually end after an hour and or two but the wars of Yugoslavia began in the early nineties and continued to be telecast for over a decade.

The question was still being asked among the children at my school. What are you? Into that definition, a space was forced open to make room for massacres and genocides, systematic rape and casual murder. Those massacres and rapes were who I was, because the television informed me that the Serbs were responsible for all the evils of those wars, and I was a Serb.

My mother wept when we watched television and hundreds of thousands of Serbs were forced from homes in Croatia, where they'd been living for generations. Many were killed and the rest forced out at gunpoint with what they could carry on trucks and trailers — or strapped to the roof of cars in teetering towers of clothes and suitcases — because the cabins of those small European cars were full of people. My mother wept as she watched the television. I'd never heard weeping before. I sat beside her and we watched the television with the volume low, an Australian voice calmly talking us through the statistics, but I was listening to the wordless noise of death and mourning from the lungs and throat of the woman sitting beside me. I saw people like me and my mother on the television. Men that resembled my father and young children who looked like my little brother. I didn't cry because I didn't know how to answer the question they were asking in school anymore. What are you?

My father, as far as his language goes, has never abandoned the shores of his homeland for longer than a few months. I became a translator before I was in my teens. I dealt with video salesmen describing features I didn't really understand and haggled over price through mumbling embarrassment with doctors, mechanics, lawyers and repair people. My Serbian was good enough to translate most of my thoughts from English, but we would never have our feet in the same country, me and my father. A language barrier that wasn't about language at all, and not even me and him, and not about Australia or its English.

It was a racial history that was being cut apart at the place he and I were connected. It wasn't a severance that slices through quickly. It was a serrated edge that moved back and forth with every passing year that we lived in Australia. I was already home but my father had not been able to travel, though he had physically moved. What was essential to him was a mystery, bound to buildings in Belgrade and caught on trees on the farm where he grew up, in a place called Jazovnik. A name I found hard to pronounce.

Some boys get the paper route. There were jobs at the local supermarket stacking shelves and collecting trolleys. I don't know what the other jobs for boys in my neighbourhood were, because mine was working in a gear-making factory. I worked there Saturdays and on school holidays, and for the most part, I liked it; thought the two dollars fifty an hour I got paid was worthwhile.

I met a man there too old to work, who told me if he stopped working he would die. They went easy on him, my father told me. Let him work a lathe that didn't much matter. A young man who worked there as well liked play-fighting with this old man who was afraid of the pointless oblivion of retirement. It was a display of strength and vigour, only one of them enjoyed. The young man one lunch break laughed about how much of his thumb he had stuck up the old guy's arse. Another factory worker there could quote Shakespeare, but maybe the only two lines I heard him use. *Our lack is nothing but our leave.* He translated that for me as meaning we need to get out of here as quickly as possible. But I didn't mind being there. I disliked getting hauled out of bed at five thirty in the morning, but I loved the fresh cinnamon doughnuts from the just-open bakery on the way to work.

We drove to the factory with whatever music I wanted to put into the tape player—mostly stuff I'd taped from Kasey Kasem's Top Forty Count Down, broadcast weekly from somewhere in the United States of America. Never once was I able to get my father to say whether he liked a particular song, or hated it. The only thing I had to remember was to turn the music off when we drove past the cemetery, where no-one was buried that we had ever known. It wasn't a lesson, of respect for the dead for instance, but more like the wordless observance of a fundamental principle that couldn't be articulated with anything other than the wordless observance itself.

Another man who worked in that Spotswood factory had burn marks all over his muscled arms. He talked to me about

God as if divinity was a wonderful thing he'd discovered one morning, waking up, a sunrise that had just broken through his whole mind. He was not trying to sell me on anything or convert me. Just tried to explain what it felt like to discover you had a soul. Something that had illuminated him with a saint-light I could see when he began talking, or worked at his machine during the long hours of his shift. It was the reason he had all the tattoos burned off his body, knowing it would be painful, and knowing it would leave appalling marks of melted flesh.

I don't remember his name, or any of their names, but I recall happiness in pulling on the blue, oil-stained coveralls. I drifted through their world and I'd now be nameless to them as well. I made little metal dowels some days and went off to the local take-away store to get everyone's food. The Heart Attack Special for the boss. Hot dogs, that were about the best thing around, for myself. My father brought his own lunch from home, mostly rye breads and salami, fresh tomatoes and fruit. He didn't come into the cafeteria to eat with the rest of us. He remained at his post, watching his machine do its work while he ate. Some type of immense lathe, set on stage, with mysterious sheets of blueprint paper arrayed around him, figures and graphs only he knew how to decipher. He looked like the high priest engineer of the whole Industrial Revolution up in that revolving metal altar. Making gears, metres wide in diameter, for power stations around Australia.

I walked out of that place every Saturday afternoon at about two or three because it was still the short day of labour in those days. I was liberated into the world of light, smelling of iron, shavings of metal in my hair, grimy with oil smudges across my face, like chimney sweeps from ten generations back. But it was real work with real money I had earned in a yellow pay packet, with a slip of calculated hours to dollars, same as everyone else's. And I wouldn't have preferred a paper route job, not then, and not now. In all of it there was another wordless observance.

There's a feature of old Yugoslavia that was still alive when I was growing up, and who knows, maybe they still do it today in those countries that spilled out of the union. Or maybe they've become like the rest of us who dance in our single spots on a dance floor, or share the half embrace of a couple rocking side to side for the slow songs. The music of those Yugoslavs was a wild thing of trumpets and drums and piano-accordions, hell bent for joy from first note to last. And every person on the dance floor held hands as they danced in the weaving circles they made. All of them danced, until they sweated through their shirts and dripped to the dust-jumping wooden floorboards. There were the old, children, teens, the middle-aged and those who hobbled when they walked. Those who led from the end of the connected hands waved a red handkerchief as a kind of exuberant flag, while the women let out screams of bliss that was the pure pleasure of the circle dance called the Kolo. The dance was thousands of years long in tradition, generation after generation of these people who were the Yugoslavs. It was true for the Macedonians, the Serbians, the Croatians, the Slovenes and the Bosnians. I danced that Kolo with them all.

Walking back from school, there are two boys who have it in their heads that I'll be their victim. No particular reason. No particular cause. Just a solidarity of two knowing that one, alone, is almost nothing. That my fear and their confidence will allow for the practice of power. The playing of domination

70

and submission as natural as bat and ball. I don't know why I remember their names, but I do. Steve Mountanen and Eric Bakka.

I don't recall the words, but it's an unrestrained ridicule that has no sense to it. It's intensely personal and directed, but also unconscious. And I keep walking, wanting to get home from school, to hide from my fear, and get away from these two, and the spite, but one of them pushes me in the shoulder, and without knowing what will happen next, I turn around with fists flying ready to fight both of them. I had found a readiness to die. Nothing childish about it or the blood that was in it. Their expression read like two boys having fun kicking a ball around when all of a sudden an adult comes into the game, roars at them, and takes the ball away. A skinny little kid, clearly afraid, and always quiet — wasn't supposed to turn around throwing punches like that.

Years later I would stand and take Croatian birthday punches in high-school, full pelt strikes to the shoulder from a Croatian boy two years older. I took those punches and showed nothing of the numbness in my arm tingling down to my fingertips, because they were ostensibly just birthday punches. Despite the fear of fighting, I wanted to show him I was strong enough to take his hardest punches without flinching. There would be more fights, all of them ones I'd done all I could do to avoid. Somehow I didn't lose any of them. As afraid as I was, there was always a point in me that, once reached, would keep going to that same feeling of blood and death that I first felt that day walking home from school with those two Aussie boys.

I fought a Croatian boy, (who had announced to our geography teacher, proudly, that all Serbs should be drowned in the Adriatic Sea), surrounded by thirty or forty other boys from our school. A showdown I could do nothing to avoid, but we threw our punches and had the stupid cheers of our school mates, the hungry spectacle of them all standing there, making sure that the wavering wills of child combatants did not result in something cowardly, and for the sake of the show, we stood face on and took our punches, until I brought his head down into the upthrust of my knee. I watched the blood spill down his face. I pushed through the cluster of boys, the victor. Walking away, stumbling home from school again, crying, and feeling nothing, nothing at all, but how terrible it was to be forced to fight.

I went to a multicultural high-school in Melbourne's western suburbs, so it was natural for the Anglo-Saxon teacher in our first geography class to go around the class and ask us all to announce what our background was. There were children from Greece, Malta, the Philippines, Argentina, Turkey, Italy, and it was a simple answer. But every child that came from Yugoslavia was a prophet, nominating countries yet to exist, such as Macedonia and Croatia. When it came my turn, filled with some kind of embarrassment that flushed my face red and drowned my voice to a whisper, I answered as my parents had told me, Yugoslavia. The geography teacher did not dispute the prophets. Didn't see a contradiction in what I told her.

For the next few years, while Yugoslavia still existed, the same was always true, and it was a safe assumption that if someone told you they were Yugoslav, they were from Serbia. This despite the fact that Serbia lost most through the Federation, and would continue to lose, until today, where perhaps the final bill to be paid is some ten percent of her territory, with the loss of Kosovo.

The pain of this division will continue as the remaining Serbs are gradually forced from Kosovo — the region in which the people that call themselves Serbian were formed. The places they built their first villages and towns have been taken away. The land where they built churches and monasteries, where they made cemeteries and mourned the passing of mothers and fathers, friends, and their children. Where they felt their ancestry growing in the soil and their heritage raised up on the branches of their culture. The churches and monasteries of Kosovo will soon be destroyed and the ground will be dug up for other bones to be buried.

The first time I remember my mother crying was when Josip Broz Tito passed away. The father of her nation had died. I don't remember my mother crying again until she wept at the forced exodus of almost a million Serbs from Croatia. Neither she or my father ever spoke with hatred for any of the people of their homeland. I did not experience the anger or animosity of those wars at home. There was nothing but a heartbreak that cannot be understood unless it is compared to the end of a romance. The heartbreak at the death of a nation.

It's an interesting question, but one that will never yield an easy answer. The elements that bind people or separate them are at root still underneath the skin. Such things come from a genetic package none of us get to open. We live for the most part oblivious to these superficialities, and hope for good lives, lived amongst our fellows as one of their number. The children in that geography class might have gone to war with each other based on the results of equations they themselves had little say in. We can all simply watch the results of these secret sums bundled up somewhere below the flesh.

Some nations have a motto. America is the home of the brave, land of the free. The French have their liberty, equality and fraternity. On the Serbian flag, inlaid into the coat of arms derived from the Kingdom of Serbia, is the letter C, repeated four times, around the cross at its centre. The Cyrillic for S, those four letters stand for *only united will the Serb be saved*. It's our way of saying, together we stand, divided we fall, but I've always been struck by the choice of that word — Saved. Where other countries proclaim and pronounce grand ideals, I am descended from a nation of people who knew that survival itself was never assured, and I live in a country which refuses to become a republic, because we don't see a need for it. Australia is young, and free.

Wars are measured in atrocities. Battle begins with the deaths of soldiers, and leads to deaths in their families, particularly when the battlefield is the neighbourhood they all live in. The murder of one person should appal us when a life is wasted over an idea of territory or a choice of God. Yet wars are not unnatural. Wars have never ceased, from our tribes and villages, to our cities and nations. Wars fought for oil in the name of Democracy are easier to accept when the battles are far from home and the victims can remain nameless and faceless.

History is a machine that was built to calculate the numbers of the dead as the rolling figures of a lottery. We watch the results when they roll into numbers in that hand-crafted machine, built as soon as we invented spears and knives. The loss of one life — the first man, woman or child — for the sake of real-estate or a method of worship, is the first atrocity. We built the machine, not to calculate the figures of the lost, mutilated or raped, but to remove the burden from our souls. When enough have suffered for useless causes we begin to live in that machine like ghosts lost in the numbers, mesmerised by the turning gears of time.

There's a kind of sad love. One that makes us feel bereft. That makes our love seem sweeter for the bitterness it comes with. It's some kind of blues we sing when everything that could have been one way, and that should have been full and whole, gets broken into bits and pieces, spills its contents, and loses its taste in the grit of the floor. There's still the song, no matter what else happens, and the sad love that it allows us to feel again, and remember what it was to hold hands in long rampaging lines, all of us calling out to each other in the bliss of the dance.

The Frame

4.

We're holding hands; thumb moving back and forth over a wrist at pulse point. A steady movement. A lazy beat. We do not stop gently. It's a full length motion picture, running on — reel to reel — to a cut frame. It lands on the floor in something less than a whisper. All the while the sound of the projector whirls along, a flickering light through no lens, onto a screen no-one's watching. It's me in an empty auditorium. With that one frame I don't know what it is we've seen and heard. Only the last frame remains. The green of a tennis court. Late at night and empty. There's no sound in that auditorium but I can still feel the twist of metal against breaking bone.

2.

The world is moving through the windows. Inside the car we listen to music from a tape that has been chewed up once or twice. There are rough sections and a chance that the car's tape-player will catch and chew it up again. The music will be deleted from my memory. What music do we listen to now? What's playing? The conversation will get all chewed up. I can hear the static, but there are hours in the cabin of this car, multiplied by days, weeks, months and years. We travel along together, talking and talking — listening to the sound of each other's voices — music playing for us in the background. We are travelling from our past into our future for such a long time.

3.

Everything's an accident. We think *destiny* and *fate* even when we don't use those words. Even when these ideas have been driven from our minds like the lie of a flat world and God smiling down at us from the white lounge chairs of heaven. Greeks gaze into empty coffee cups and look into the smudge of chaos like scientists who stare through their microscopes at a smear of cells — but they're the same stains. Accidents of birth, followed by accidents of life and then accidents of death. We collide into the people we marry, and the collision might spill out children… or nothing much at all, when you can't read the messages in smudges and smears.

1.

We come around the bend along Kings Way, heading away from the city. To our right is a golf course and its high wire fencing, and beyond that, the lake. The swans of Albert Park, and their trailing cygnets, dozing as they drift across the cold black starflecked water. There's a restaurant beside the lake that we like. We celebrated my 21st birthday there on a night where a lot of us got drunk and a girl with a champagne voice whispered something heady into my ear. For hours later, there was the corrosive of jealousy poured into the same ear to clean it out; of other voices and their whispered threats to our love. To the left, is a tennis court, with night lights, though it's too late for anyone to be playing. The green of the court, with its net and a tired white chord dipping in the middle.

Back when Jean-Michel Basquiat was My Best Friend

Back in the day (when I wore a New York soul like a Bowery whore wears stolen mink) Jean-Michel would tell me my eyes were the colour of Greenwich Village in the summer, when vendors trundled along the cracked, hot sidewalks, selling ices. The emerald lime flavour wasn't his favourite but didn't it look genius with a backdrop of worn out metal and concrete?

He took me around the city, showing me the choice graffiti, and explained that if they hadn't designed such soulless architecture, there wouldn't be a need for the adornments of our spray-painted words. He said, to be a master of this metropolis you need to have lived for a few seasons in a cardboard box in Central Park.

Jean-Michel walked in front of me in that slow jive patter, where his feet dwelt on curbs like gentle fingertips upon the shoulders of a fond friend.

I think about his slow hopes, lazy desires, relentless need, lacerating dreams and how they curled up on the dirty carpet of a brownstone; Jean-Michel rolled up his beautiful eyes and saw nothing more. I want to say that a city with a broken heart need not cost the life of a paint-spattered visionary. That New York should not forget seduction so soon after it is drowned in kisses.

I told him maybe it was time to leave Gotham and find a place where art was allowed to grow old but he was not really listening as we walked along angry Cuban streets. We weaved through girls on roller-skates and headphones singing songs by Madonna with Latin accents.

We went to a bar and he told the barman we were best buddies back from when we were both a gleam in the same Brooklyn milkman's eye. The barman told me he had Jean-Michel design him his first tattoo, that he loved it so much, he got Jean-Michel to design enough of them to cover his entire body. Now his wife opens him like a scroll every evening and loves every line and crease of his flesh. In the past, they had fought over things like what shade of white to paint the walls of a tenement they could barely afford. These days they just made love whenever the New York orchestra of car horns and sirens reached a crescendo. Jean-Michel drinks for free here, the barman said, and so should his best friend.

There was Polish vodka with a long thin blade of grass in the bottle, cranberry juice, and a big stainless steel bowl of lime wedges we squeezed into the cut crystal glasses ourselves. We got drunk and he told me that every cent he ever made from the canvas was the opposite of what he'd done for the barman and his well loved flesh. All the images got sharper in Jean-Michel's mind and his flesh seemed more cut up by the dollar.

Writing graffiti on the walls of the city had filled him with the upward rush of Manhattan. The occasional crumbs of concrete in his shoes or a leaf in his hair from a park now just made him want to sleep in the subways again. Jean-Michel said the trains moved billions, through all this city's relentless seasons (but twenty-seven is such a cruel number when counting out your trips around the sun). When he wrote on the walls, bridges and city doors, the metropolis charged him with its ambition, its colossal creation and its brief salvation.

He leaned forward so that he could look me in that Big Apple soul I mentioned earlier, and he drawled in that soft, careful way, as though he was wielding a loving razor with his tongue, the lovely lie about my Greenwich eyes and ice, flavoured emerald green, eaten when we were lost children roaming the streets in New York summers.

The Amsterdam Keyhole

J & K had a real deal romance. It started all the way back when she was sixteen and kept his scarf wrapped around her neck—not because it was cold but because she wanted to smell him all day at school. Her picture went into his wallet, though he'd never done that before. He took out the photobooth black & white to show people at work his pretty new girlfriend. J & K knew it was the real deal. They bought each other good gold rings from a jeweller in the city and put them on their wedding fingers. No priests or churches. No family and friends. Both decided that's the way it should be. They never once thought it was strange to throw themselves—mind, body and soul—into death-do-us-part vows.

They watched a lot of films together but they didn't go to parties or do things with other couples. J & K moved deeper into each other for five years. It was as though they'd found the secret to everything. Two was enough—Beginning all the way to the End. A very large nutshell for their cosy universe.

K worked in a mail centre, sorting letters, while J studied at university. She taught him about Frieda Kahlo. They went to exhibitions. They talked about how Klimt used to paint everyone naked before he clothed them in all that resplendent colour. J painted every now and then. They were dark, contorted shapes she put to canvas but she never showed many people; not even him. K read a lot, but J wasn't interested in his books. He wrote poetry he didn't let anyone see. K didn't write about love and when he showed J the pages, she shuffled through them because it was only his love she wanted to see.

K was nineteen when he met J. It was not a long wait compared to some, who wait far longer, and in the waiting, let it go as mostly myth. But he had waited long enough to feel love turning into all kinds of lies. Dried out flies, on a window ledge, that never opened.

J & K liked to get dressed up and go to expensive restaurants though neither of them earned a lot of money or knew much about fine dining. The clothes they bought were the slightest bit like costumes. They talked about the future and settled on all the names of their daughters and sons. They looked at each other in those bright city restaurants and believed that what everyone else at all the other tables wished for and hoped they had, was already found and belonged to J & K forever. It wasn't a fairytale. It hadn't passed away after a few months into some silliness of youth.

They went to the Ballet and were almost comfortable in their new clothes, bought especially for the evening. The dancers came out and K was surprised that it was possible to hear their feet hitting the polished wood of the stage during some movements. J & K kissed during intermission, as everyone else drifted out for drinks, or to the ladies and gents. They stayed in their seats and the emptying theatre filled them with the world's dreams. They kissed and there was nothing else. The people to whom the theatre more properly belonged, returned to their seats and didn't notice J & K at all. A moment had passed but no-one felt anything other than the vibration of the air as the orchestra began to play again.

J & K decided to go to Europe. They took their gold rings off before they left but they told each other nothing had changed. They travelled in trains from city to city and they made love everywhere they went. By the time they came to Amsterdam they'd almost run out of money. They bought exotic sounding cannabis and smoked it in the Red Light District. K was appalled by the shop-front prostitutes and the way men walked in, brought out their wallets from a back pocket, and paid—the curtain pulled only at the last moment. J was untroubled. She walked around with a hard grin. She saw it all as a vast Klimt painting before the layers of gold and silver and jewels went on and covered these naked bodies all around them.

They were out of time. In a few days they'd be catching a flight back to Melbourne. They sat in a cheap hamburger joint. Smoked the last of the Amsterdam grass and laughed like very young children with the giggles.

They were laughing as they tried to kiss but couldn't get sober enough for their lips to form the right shapes. Their teeth clinked against each other instead. In the lulls between the laughter, K could feel his lungs vibrating with the next wave of laughter about to break through him. His heart taking big gulps of blood in preparation.

J stopped laughing. She had an odd smile on her pretty face. She stood between his legs and her breasts pushed back his face a millimetre. K wouldn't have moved. He would have closed his eyes but J bent down, and instead of kissing him, she placed a thumb and forefinger, above and below his eye. She peered down, as though looking through a keyhole.

J & K stepped out of that Amsterdam hamburger joint. K remembered that moment at the Ballet, the full silence as everyone hushed and waited for the orchestra to play. He felt the same burgeoning hush. J & K walked to the hostel they were staying in, through a neighbourhood of houseboats, floating on Amsterdam's canals. J & K felt good as they walked to the hostel they were staying in.

'You know I love you, right?' Jennifer had declared her love to Kevin many times in the last five years. But it was the first time, at that moment, that Kevin didn't believe her.

I Wanna be Murakami

I used to be happy. Tolstoy tells me I shouldn't have sex. Henry Miller tells me I should get more; to be experimental and maybe even rough. But I like the way Murakami kisses. Not the author himself (since he's kind of ugly) but his lovely characters. I could watch them kissing all day. Every book comes with a soundtrack and bad things might happen but it's alright when they do.

It's not like when I nailed my hand to a wooden beam with my new nail gun. I was left hanging there for hours. I didn't have my mobile with me and there was no-one around. I could have shouted out or screamed, and perhaps a neighbour in one of the adjoining flats would have heard me, but I have a dreadful fear of looking like an idiot.

Maybe I would have starved to death hanging from the nail in the beam, but I fell off the ladder. They put stitches that resembled a Japanese word in my hand — that's what gave me the idea that life as Murakami would have been so much better than the life of A.S. Patrić.

I'm sad all the time now. Hanging from my nail, I imagined all those Japanese women kissing me on the lips. Some closing their eyes and others keeping them open. Some smelling as nice as well groomed fluffy cats and others smiling like drowsy kittens looking for a puddle of sunlight to nap in.

I was hanging there for hours and I felt kind of lonely. There was no soundtrack music to the book I was writing and no-one wanted to magically appear at my window.

While I was hanging by that nail I wondered about what Anais Nin would have kissed like. Anais kissed famous women and notorious men; kissed people that tasted of mint leaves in Cuban bars; kissed under tables in Parisian restaurants and in the alleyways of Barcelona; in New York art galleries, and she would have kissed me like a Jackson Pollock painting.

Things like that happen to Murakami. Anais would have been strolling by my window and then she would have walked right in and pulled the nail out with her pearl white teeth. She had a small feline face and it would have been easy for her. Maybe then she would've spat out that long nasty nail and kissed me.

Thoughts of kissing Anais now only bring me sadness because she's off to different stories like she was never anything more than a character in other people's minds. I know that's not true and that there were months on the Seine, in a houseboat, where she dreamed about men like me wanting to kiss her. I've got a pain in my hand thinking about it.

I suppose when something bad happens, like accidentally firing a nail into the back of your hand with a nail gun, you hope that whatever angels you have floating around your soul, will come to console and make you feel like you're not alone in the universe with your sadness. I wish Anais Nin could've shown up at my window, if only to wave, but she didn't. I know if I was Murakami that would have been possible.

Ducks

There's a smell in the air that neither of them wants to mention. Two or three gnats roam the beams of sunlight pushing through the still air of the kitchen. No-one opens the windows anymore because no-one can reach them.

Some days there's not much to say so they listen to Anais's house creaking. June lives a street away in a semi-detached. On the other side of the party wall there's a couple with babies, toddlers and rampaging boys. June says it's like living with a large colony of possums in the walls.

June comes to visit Anais often. They sit and June says it's a lovely sound the house makes as it creaks. Anais says it's the house settling. June points out that it's been twenty years now that Anais has been living here, and forty before that it's stood, and all that time settling without being settled—that's a fair amount of restless energy.

The arthritic dog next door begins barking blindly, going berserk at falling leaves or at memories of plucky paper boys cutting across fresh lawns with their bicycles. He doesn't have the wind to keep it up for long.

"You know, I've been thinking," June says. "There's nothing special about here—this place. Who cares where you live? No-one talks to anyone. There's no sense of community any more. It must be the same kind of thing a dog feels when you throw him in someone's backyard for long enough. He thinks he loves it, so he defends it. I just wound up in Elwood and I patrol these streets like they mean something to me." She tugs a plastic-wrapped package of cigarettes out of her handbag. "But God, I do love this place."

Anais lifts the mug full of bourbon to her face, drinks, coughs, puts it down. "I don't care about any of that. You're just talking to hear yourself talk."

June scratches through her thin white hair; feels her pink scalp beneath her fingers. "I think I'm going bald." Cups her gigantic, sagging breasts, lifts them like she was at the market and wants to test the weight of cantaloupes, "And these things keep on growing. Why? Getting this old is like stepping off the genetic map. My earlobes are going to touch my shoulders soon."

Anais takes another loud sip from her mug. "No wonder no-one wants to speak to you any more. You should talk about sensible things; like the Olympics. You should watch the swimming."

"The swimming? They should have people like me swimming, and then I'd watch. These young, half-naked seals all look alike. Why should I care? They've got people winning for Australia. I want someone to win for Elwood." June taps the pack of cigarettes, which she bought on her morning walk from the 7-Eleven on the corner of Broadway and Ormond. She taps them on the kitchen table for a few reflective seconds. She unwraps the plastic and realises she forgot to buy a lighter or matches. "I need something to light these." She talks around the long white cylinder of tobacco.

"You don't smoke," Anais tells June.

"I used to smoke. I was a chimney," June tells Anais.

"When?" Anais asks, putting down her mug with two hands. "When were you ever a chimney?"

 The Rattler & other stories

"Forty years ago. No use fighting the inevitable though. Once a smoker, always a smoker. The Olympics make me want to smoke."

"I'm not giving you a lighter. This is stupid." Anais finishes her mug of bourbon. "And to tell you the truth, I'm feeling… shame-faced. Drinking with you on a Sunday morning, when I should probably be at church or the library. I should be respectable by now."

"You should be vacuuming this floor. Look at the lino. It's disgusting." June says.

Anais refuses to look down at the kitchen floor. "What are you talking about? It's not disgusting. You and your giant breasts propped on my kitchen table are disgusting."

"I brought over a bag of salt-and-vinegar chips last week," June says, "and I spilt some of the crumbs from the bottom of the bag. And there they are."

"You didn't come over last week."

"Well, the week before that. Which is even worse."

"I think they're crumbs from something else. I had nachos the other night."

June gets up and begins hunting in the messy kitchen drawers for a lighter. "I want to get back to my point." She opens and closes cupboard doors, finds a half-eaten sandwich on a plate in one of them. In the oven there's a burned bird carcass—charcoal, with a beak still on it. Gnats erupt from the open oven door.

Anais waves at June to shut it.

"You look like you're about to take flight," June tells Anais. She lifts a hand to her mouth. "What's my point?" she asks.

"People like you competing at the Olympics, for Elwood. Ridiculous."

"Don't you say anything bad about Elwood. I love this neighbourhood. They don't like to speak over the fences anymore. It doesn't matter. It's still Elwood."

"You should find one of those shirts. 'I heart Elwood'." Anais shoos away a few gnats orbiting her head like a miniature solar system.

"I'd buy one, I'll tell you that for nothing. But I hate it when people say I 'heart' anything. It's I 'love' something. Like it never used to be 'I heart N.Y.' but 'I love New York', and now it's 'I heart Frankston'. What's going on? Are the dyslexics taking over the world?" June finds a box of matches on top of the fridge, hunts through black burned out matches to get one that's still got a red tip.

"What about 'I heart silence?'" Anais takes the bottle of bourbon from under the table and pours herself another half-mug. "What about 'I heart euthanasia?'"

"I want to keep the machines on. For as long as possible. Don't believe it when they tell you I'm brain dead. I'm in there somewhere."

"As if anyone is going to ask me. They won't bother with machines for you. They hate smokers. It even makes your toes rot now. I've seen pictures. These days they'd pour something combustible over you and light a match."

"I don't believe in cremation. You can't put people in ovens, give someone a thingamajig full of ashes. They expect you to take it home. I don't want someone's remains on the top of my fridge. They should give you a commemorative ashtray at least." Holding up the lit cigarette, "Where do I ash this?"

Anais levers herself semi-erect, and moves crablike along the kitchen table and out of the room, returning a few moments later with a white plastic ashtray, the blue and red stripes around its radius faded, its centre embossed with the Footscray Football

Club logo. A snarling bulldog looks up through old black smoulder marks.

June looks at the bulldog and feels sorry for him. Thrown in there like that. The people who love Footscray should not be putting out their cigarettes on him. Where's the club loyalty in that? They should have used the little blue boy of Carlton Football Club for the Footscray fans. Or the magpies. The eagles and swans. The whole menagerie. But why this poor dog, who only wanted to defend something?

"You look like you're about to cry," Anais says. "Don't think about cremation. Someone has to want cremation. They don't put you in an oven like a Sunday roast."

"I don't like worms any better. I don't like the idea of them crawling around in there with their hungry little mouths. I don't even like gardening. If they could just think of a better way." Her eyes follow the ribbon of cigarette smoke up to the mould-spotted ceiling. "I'd prefer just to vanish."

"Maybe the next time they're testing a nuclear weapon they could put you underneath it," Anais suggests.

"Are you losing your marbles? Australia doesn't have nuclear weapons."

"Well… we should. At least a few of them. Have you seen how many American tourists there are these days? They want to take over."

"I don't want a nuclear explosion, in any case. That's just like ashes, but smaller. I like the idea of evaporation. Like a dream rising from the pillows of my bed," June smiles—she's always thought of herself as a poetic soul.

"That's the way it was with Henry," says Anais. "He had a smile on his face. And an erection. It was wonderful. He must have been thinking of me when he died. He always said I was cream and his taste of paradise this side of the Milky Way."

"That's a quote," June says, upstaged. It sounds spiteful even to her own ears but she can't help it.

"That's not a quote. He could be poetic," Anais says, almost getting out of her chair.

"Probably someone good, like Hemingway." June taps her ash into the ashtray.

Anais slams a hand down on the table for dramatic effect, but clips her mug and scrambles to save it from falling to the floor.

She's spluttering, "Hemingway? You can't be serious. Hemingway didn't even like women. He wouldn't have known the taste of cream if you put a warm spoon of it to his lips. Didn't know cream from bream. That's why he needed to put some shotgun ventilation into his skull. That old man and his sea—" Anais chokes on the angry words racing from her mouth, and without a chance to breathe goes pale, her eyelids trembling.

She takes another sip of the good bourbon June brought her. Because June knows how much she loves bourbon.

June takes a breath, and blinks. Blinks, and takes another breath. "I swim the twenty-five metre pool every week. I'm still in good condition."

She does breast stroke—and backstroke if she's really feeling up for it—twice a week at the St Kilda Sea Baths. She has a red rubber cap that says 'Elwood' in black letters along each side of it.

She keeps it on in the spa after her swims, and looks out at the flat water of Port Phillip Bay, feeling the romance of sails whenever she sees them out there; but she also likes the immense freight ships moving towards the setting sun, and the heavy promise of return they press across the lips of the horizon.

Henry got the swimming cap as a secret birthday present for June many years ago. Sometimes she puts it on and walks around the neighbourhood, but she doesn't like the looks she gets.

Anais says, "Take that cigarette out of your mouth. You're not even inhaling."

"I had this dream last night," says June. "I was walking along Addison Street and about to cross the canal when I noticed there were all these ducks floating out to sea. There were thousands of them on the smelly canal water, and all of them were wearing gold medals. They were quacking the Australian national anthem, all together. It sounded terrible. As I sat there on the edge of the canal, I realised I was an old duck, and I didn't have a medal because I wanted to compete for Elwood, and everybody'd thought that was stupid."

Anais waves a hand at the gnats still orbiting her head. She wonders why they don't seem to bother with June. "This is just shameful. And ridiculous."

"If you still had a man, shameful would still be a nice word. But you might as well be a virgin again. You probably are. You've grown a new hymen by now."

"Virgin? Me? I'll have you know that I got around back in my day. I was game for anything. Big Boy Joe Batty said I had 'a healthy appetite'. That's what he said, shaking his head in disbelief and wonder." All Anais' Ss are turning into slivery things her thick tongue doesn't fancy any more.

She looks into her mug and remembers Joe, with his paint-spattered overalls that could resemble the night sky in a dimly lit room, and his huge hands that could crush an empty tuna can (she'd seen him do it) but had the delicacy of touch on her body to rival a violinist's caress.

"Healthy appetite! He was probably referring to all the nacho eating."

"They didn't have nachos in those days."

"Of course they did. Nachos. They've been around for… since before Elwood."

"The pizzas were still in Italy. The souvlakia still in Greece. And all of that stuff was still in Mexico. We had fish and chips. No smelly dim sims or crappy Chico-Rolls either. Just fresh fish in batter and chips the size of Olympic gold medals."

They fall into a silent contemplation of these changes. There are pictures of Anais' husbands on the walls and in grimy photo frames arrayed on the dusty furniture. All of them done in by bad hearts. Something to do with the kind of love Anais put into them, June is sure. Each in their reign had exclusive rights to the walls and furniture of Anais' house. As the years of their absence went on, they seemed to have congregated, shoulder to shoulder, in the friendly fellowship of her ring. As though there is one happy bed made for all four of them in the hereafter.

June looks at Henry, smiling at her from the wall, from just below the dead kitchen clock (whose hands haven't moved in the ten years since Anais was last able to get onto a chair to replace its battery), and smiles back up at him. A sweet smile he would remember even in heaven. A smile that belongs to him alone.

Anais' simmering silence finally breaks and she bursts out, "You have never gotten over the fact that, in the end, Henry chose me. Not you. Me!" Anais grabs the black-and-white photograph of her first husband off the wall and places it between them on the kitchen table. Henry looks up at the ceiling, a wink in his eye directed at God or the clouds above.

"What makes you think he chose? Did he choose?" June asks, stubbing out her cigarette. "Maybe he couldn't choose." She feels her heart vibrating in her chest. She can almost feel Henry on the table, his big rolling laughter that made her want to drown in it.

"What are you talking about now?" Anais leans back, her last shout turning into a wheezy puff. Her eyes narrow, closing with two deep blinks.

Anais and June's ominous silence lasts for almost ten minutes.

June finally lights another cigarette and says, "A real estate agent keeps telling me how good property values are now for houses in Elwood. She thinks I'm sitting on a fortune. 'A golden egg', she calls it."

Anais opens her eyes wide, "But this is Elwood. Where else could you live?"

June nods, watching her cigarette smoke rise around her. "That's what I'm saying. I tell her that, every time she calls. This is Elwood."

Jiggling the Molecules

Michelle's school folders were covered in slashes of Texta. Bands she liked. Singers she loved. The lyrics made it to her flesh in Biro tattoos, up and down her forearms, the ink pressed down with as much permanence as she could manage. There were pictures and posters in her locker of bands like *Uncanny X-men* and Brian Mannix. Michelle was always singing—the voices of beautiful men under her breath. I told her I wanted to cut my hair like one of the guys from *Duran Duran* and she thought they were cool as well.

Michelle's friend Amy told us her parents were away for the weekend and we could come over on Sunday to listen to *Purple Rain*. I was thrilled to be invited to come along. To enter a strange house and to sit in someone's lounge to listen to music on a proper stereo. Amy brought out chips and soft drinks. We spoke about films we'd seen like *American Werewolf in London* and shows we liked watching on TV. Michelle talked about *21 Jump Street*. She was infatuated with Johnny Depp. I murmured that he wasn't real and she couldn't really be in love with a heart-throb in America. We talked about teachers we hated and kids in school that had done stupid things. But nothing I said or did made a difference. None of it got me beyond the elusive periphery of Michelle's attention. There was a knock at the door. We didn't have to wonder who it was. I'd already told them I'd invited my friend Anton.

He was a year or two older but he didn't go to Kealba High with us. He didn't even go to High School. He went to the local Tech. It was a mystery what kind of school that was. Mostly boys. Tough. There were daily fights over there and they studied trades like carpentry and plumbing. But Anton didn't seem like he'd been in a lot of fights and there was nothing about the Trades in the way he looked. He'd done everything he could manage to look like Jon Bon Jovi. He pulled it off as though it was the most natural thing in the world. He didn't need the guitar, band or songs. Anton walked into the room and everything changed. It wasn't an after school get-together any more. It was something else. I didn't know what, but there was no mistaking the change in atmosphere.

Anton and Michelle both had things they said over and again, without realising it. Michelle said, "Up here for thinking, down there for dancing." Anton liked to say, "Let's go and jiggle the molecules." Marlon Brando used to say that to his friends and Anton had picked it up on a television doco. It meant having a good time. It meant sneaking into night clubs and drinking. It meant having sex. There was still a difference between that and fucking. A subtle one that was changing even in that suburban house.

When Anton walked into that loungeroom he made us feel like children at a stupid kid's birthday party, eating Twisties, drinking Fanta and listening to Prince. I'm not sure how much thought Michelle put into what she meant with her mantra. Maybe it was a lyric by Brian Mannix, or a sound bite from an interview. She told Anton she loved to dance and Anton sat down on the couch and lit a cigarette. He said, "Alright. Dance."

In Science they taught us the air was a gas. Not the Nothing that it seemed to be. I could feel myself breathing in that kind of heavy air. I watched Michelle dancing by herself in the loungeroom to the song *Darling Nikki*. Amy left to get an ashtray from the kitchen so that Anton wouldn't ash on the carpet. I didn't know what was wrong but there was something broken about Michelle's movements. I wanted to close my eyes or turn the stereo off, but I sat next to Anton and watched Michelle dance. The air swirled around her like it was turning into a gas she could swim through. If Anton lit another match the whole room would explode. But he smoked his cigarette quietly, and before she was done dancing for us, he got up and left the room.

We weren't sure where he was going but staying in the lounge afterwards seemed impossible. The sudden intoxication sent us reeling down the corridors. When we walked past Amy's bedroom I told Michelle I needed to say something to her. We went in there and I closed the door. The curtains were drawn in Amy's room, as they were everywhere else in the house. It might have been the way Amy's parents preferred it but maybe Amy pulled them shut because we were coming over. Amy's bed was small. Her parents had bought it for a much younger Amy. The stuffed animals piled into a corner, head over tail, probably still had a home on her bed when kids from school weren't coming around. Michelle and I looked through Amy's records. She had a good collection. *Thriller, Madonna* (the self titled first album) and *Born in the USA* among them. Michelle and I looked at the records. Michelle said Springsteen sucked and I told her I loved her and I wrapped my arms around her and tried to kiss her.

There was a park nearby. Anton and Michelle sat on a park bench. I had spoken to Anton about Michelle. He said he didn't see anything in Michelle but I think he felt the allure she had in my eyes. The love I had for her was confessed and pledged through him, as to a confessor who knew the mysteries of this kind of god. I knew he'd understand what could be done with such a love. One that plagued the mind on waking, and troubled the sleep beforehand, and riddled the days after, until everything was upside down and inside out.

Amy and I sat on another bench trying to find something to talk about. I told Amy I really loved Springsteen, especially *Born to Run*, but she hadn't heard it yet. Amy said she loved Springsteen as well and then asked me if I wanted to go watch *Desperately Seeking Susan* with her next weekend. I couldn't even pretend that was likely to happen. We watched our lead actors lean into each other on that park bench and kiss. We watched them move closer and embrace. We watched them get up and move deeper into the park until Amy got up and said she had to go. I sat on that park bench by myself, not knowing what to do. I felt like I'd fallen over and broken some ribs. I took shallow breaths and thought about how they'd only met because of me.

Anton called out from behind trees, foliage and grass; from somewhere in the park. After a few moments, I heard him call out to me again. I followed his voice through to a small natural alcove between low hanging trees. He was lying on top of Michelle. She was lying on bark—the backs of her wrists pressed down beside her head. She didn't struggle against the arms that held her down to the rough bark beneath her wrists. She looked afraid and I could hear all three of us breathing as though we were in a small room together. A tiny space the world didn't know about. She wasn't afraid that Anton was going to do something to her, as much as she was that he'd just get off her, and leave. She didn't want me there. She didn't look at me. Anton told me to undo the buttons of her shirt. I looked at

100

Michelle and I knew she wouldn't make a sound. If this was what Anton wanted, she'd do it. I didn't want to touch Michelle. All I wanted was for her to look at me. But she was lost in that park and there was dancing in her thinking and drunken thoughts in her feet. I closed my eyes and crawled back out from beneath the low hanging trees.

I walked home along suburban footpaths. Men were watering their lawns or walking their dogs or getting into their cars or coming home from work or checking their mailboxes. Children were playing games and there were women calling them in or bringing out jumpers, or carrying them apples. The houses were shut and curtains drawn as I made my way home. A fifteen minute walk home, every step of it taken with a face wet with tears. I don't think I'd cried like that before that day. So helplessly. Passing all those houses, not even able to cover my face with my hands.

Prayers for Cracks in the Concrete

I want to talk to you. Come closer. There are so many stars above you. But none of them have ears. They won't listen. Not to say it's all silence. The first illusion of birth is separation—the first of death is silence. I'll tell you how to find the cracks. What else matters? Everything. That's the truth. There's nothing irrelevant. It's the first press of a kiss, before the lips part. Before the taste of another. There's skin wrinkling at the edges of our eyes like thousands of Christmases worth of discarded wrapping paper. Even so, we are not colourful. Sometimes there is no colour at all. Clarity in open sky blue that almost evaporates at the horizon. A place to stand. It doesn't have to be a mountain. A hill with grass growing, like grass that has never heard, never even dreamed of the obscenity of concrete. We should laugh up on that hill. But we don't need a hill. We could be flat. A pinpoint on a perfect circle billions of kilometres round. If this X marked the spot you'd never need to move. You would see the truth everywhere. That there is no flatness. The world never was flat. There's nowhere flat. Perfectly flat. Or perfectly round. Except in our minds, and then, only as a concept. Can there be truth in a concept? I'll let you decide. Like the concept of God. I pray at night. Mostly I forget. There is this desire to talk to the earless black spaces up there. To throw blood up at the soulless canvas. Before dreams perform our nightly obliteration. If it's the hungry soul of this vast bear god in the caves of our bodies, maybe it would make the difference. The hunt. Let's remember the steam from our mouths in the brittle morning, beneath limitless emerald canopies, singing above, birds on fire with vermillion and indigo. Puffs of steam in the limitless vacuum. Would it be you? Me? If not and the answer is neither, then there's unbroken concrete. What then? I imagine blades of grass. Never more than seed. We will sweat in the soil. The only prayer is for a crack—just the smallest fissure to slither our green life through. Mostly I forget. Then I remember you. I want you to remember me. Nothing's irrelevant. Everything matters. The eternally exploding stars with all that light to burn into the impossible gulfs of infinity. I wonder if they believe only in the roar of fire and light. They can't accept the concept of vacuum. I'd like that kind of bravura. Say there is no distance between you and me. You already know, without me telling you. We should not accept the perfect circle. That's what I'm thinking. Believe only in the rule of tendrils. In roots and the implacable law of the squiggle. Wave at each other like the tails of sperm. Know, like an ovum, circles are impossible. Laugh at the idea. Laugh at a continuum of vacuum. Our silent dead womb only seeming to suffocate God and his wriggling, giggling angels. Millions of blades of grass ruffling with the wind. And maybe you can tell me. I heard it's true. Or it's possible. The sound those blades make as the wind moves—don't they sing? I know it's useless talking like this. We like walking on concrete, you and me. We want it to be poured everywhere. Barefoot dreams remind you of perfect circles. More often, these are your dreams: Imprisonment. Being chased by something relentless and absolute. Teeth falling out. Kissing ghosts, evaporating in the morning. And there's longing. We stay patient, though longing is the truth. We don't know how to feast on kisses. We get bored with love. Wish, if we live long enough, wish for the death of longing. And for this kiss to be like a perfect circle. You and me. No birth. No death. Happy as God in the womb. Silent as prayers whispered in paradise. Just the stars, singing.

The Ink on Her Lips

She liked to read all the time. Writers I'd never heard of like Grace Paley and Lorrie Moore and Deborah Eisenberg. Who were these strange women coming into our house through the windows, whispering things into her ears?

Even in the bathtub. There would be fat, wet fingerprints in the margins that would warp the paper on drying. And then she did strange things with the books she didn't enjoy. There was a pile of them outside our bedroom window, soggy with rain. A jumble among the roots of our ant-infested lemon tree. She tore a book in half once, saying the author had no spine. She boiled one alive. The water went black with ink and the pages swelled until they resembled parboiled human flesh.

One of her favourite writers died. A poet that somehow had films made from her books. She called in sick because of it. I thought there was a head in the garbage when I came home in the evening. The top of someone's severed head. There was so much long black hair in the kitchen bin. Hacked swathes of it. Some strange impromptu ritual of mourning.

She didn't stop at a bob. Cut it down to concentration camp style. It revealed scars on the back of her head. One ran around the base of her skull, from ear to ear, deep and jagged. I asked her what had happened. She said she'd been pushed and fell through a window. I wondered about other ways it happened as though she was lying. I dreamed that she could open her head at this seam and liked to feed a live squirming mouse to a white owl that lived in her skull when I wasn't watching.

She used to say things that stopped me dead in my tracks. Once when we were driving she told me the rain was like words making sentences and she wanted to go outside and open her mouth so that she could taste the meaning of the ink-black spaces between the stars. She wanted to fill her mouth with it because her bones were already dry with death and thirst was part of making words. Even when they were put to paper, sentences needed the moisture of a mouth to love them into life again. They needed to be licked off the page when you were dying of thirst. The skies were spilling out from a broken ink well and God sometimes got a grip on handles like the human torso, using heads like mops or quills. She could see the wet ink of the rain and the way it was writing out the world and she just wanted to get drunk on it. I looked over at her and saw her staring outside the window and knew she was doing that in her imagination. She wasn't there in the interior warmth of the car with me. She was outside in the rain, with her face to the black, ink-stained clouds, drinking that water.

I thought at least she was interesting and we fucked like there was poetry to be found with our mouths as well. I knew she was a big reader before we moved in together but I had no idea she'd be reading me things while we slept. They say talking in your sleep is normal but different voices babbled from her mouth. There was a lot of dialogue and even some crying. The laughing was worse.

We split up not long after we moved in together. We'd been happy for the six months beforehand.

A few years went by, and I thought I'd rid myself of her forever, but then I started dreaming about her. She had the same very long hair that went wavy only in the last few inches. The same bent teeth in her bottom jaw. I took a hold of her hair like it was never a curtain to be hacked away in chunks because she needed to mourn the death of poetry with a knife. We moved through an old house. A childhood home. We kissed and grappled between furs hanging in a walk-in wardrobe, stumbling in our desperation and falling to the piles of women's shoes below the many hanging coats. The shoes smelled of leather and had sharp heels. Oh, but it's such a shame that I'm dead, she said, just before I could climax.

I began to wonder what had become of her and how she was living now. I wanted to know who she replaced me with. Was it possible she was living alone? Just her and all those writers whispering their words into her head, even when she was in the shower.

She imagined that there was a way she could open her mouth and let it fill her with streams of sentences wriggling down and around her silent throat; wishing she was made of paper. But, in the end, all she could do was spit out mouthfuls of shower water. She told me this as I brought her a clean towel, and I kissed her breasts and belly while I dried her small feet. I didn't ask her the questions that were in my mind because I couldn't understand the kinds of insanity that make a person so beautiful it makes you want to drown yourself in it.

She'd found a way to dissolve her mind in ink and what she spoke needed to be written down by someone who knew the secrets of words better than I ever will. I could only come far enough along to understand that those women writers had done more than scribble—pen to paper. That it wasn't just about the messages delivered by the hammers of typewriters or the whispering rush of printers. In her way of understanding things, she was paper for the wet ink on their lips to find final expression. That lipstick-black kiss only she could feel.

We would cook meals together and eat with half formed smiles on our faces. We'd chat about things we'd read in the newspaper or overheard on the tram in the morning. We sometimes drank beer. We would go and watch a film and it would all seem so normal I could think about drying her small feet and forget the kind of insanity she'd rained down on the back of my head like spatters of enchantment.

One day I came home and saw all those books lining the walls like skulls in a tomb and I couldn't breathe. The paper was like lengths of flesh, folded over and cut into squares, and she'd laid these out beside her bed but they were also on the floor in other rooms. I packed all the clothes I needed in a suitcase. It was an escape—not an exit.

I didn't write her a letter to explain. I had no words to tell her why all of it scared me so much. I bought a blank card and sat at the kitchen table that last day. I thought about the book she had tried to eat, one page every day, because a poet called Dorothy Porter died. I had never hit a woman before but I slapped her that day and told her to spit out the paper. Tears spilled from her swelling eyes and she wouldn't open her mouth. Later she told me the sacrifices that were made to put life into those pages couldn't be repaid. That she felt a compulsion to find another way to let the words in.

So I sat before the blank card I'd bought at a newsagency. It had a picture of a field of flowers and a tree and a quicksilver river running through the green. I realised that all the images taken together resembled an abstract face, smiling, and that it was designed to be a gift card. I couldn't find any words for her so I put it back in the envelope, planning to take it with me. Maybe I'd phone instead. I left it there and I know that was cruel.

She was a quiet woman who liked to read. A hush in her voice that was lovely when you noticed it. She was pretty enough, but especially beautiful when she slept. I remember she would begin whispering as we got ready to go to bed, before and after brushing our teeth and as we took off our clothes and put on our pyjamas. My voice would also fall to a whisper. We kissed each other every night like children and wished each other sweet dreams.

She didn't have any friends but she was invited often enough to drink or dance or talk. She preferred the books below the bed. The death of a poet hurt her. And there was nothing that should have scared me in any of that. But after my dream I couldn't bear the thought of her dead. I couldn't find a word about her on the internet or a listing in the directories, and there was no-one I could contact who knew what happened to her or where she might have gone.

I searched for those obscure writers and I read stories by them about women and the men they loved. I looked for those kinds of tales especially and I couldn't help but wonder whether I would have been a good character in one of those stories. I know I wouldn't have been. I was just the paper. A card that was left behind, an abstract face with a silver river for a mouth, and when opened, just blank like something that has never seen ink or the way it can rain.

Baby Shoes

There are nights when my wife moans like a dog. There's no story in that, the Yankee tells me, so he ignores it. He asks again about the baby shoes hanging from a nail on the wall. I like this black iron nail hammered through the concrete. You must have used a big hammer to get that nail in so deep, he says. Give me another cigarette, I tell him. No really, I'm interested in those shoes. Why do they hang on a blank wall? A big picture would obscure some of these cracks. They make your house seem poised—as though about to collapse. I tell him my wife makes the noise of a hungry street dog when I talk about such things. He laughs when I say street dog, but I think I don't talk very well.

I would prefer the sound of the ocean to speak my mind back to me when we go out on the water to fish. Except that the Yankee is always talking. He talks about baseball, and women, and asks me about knife fights I have seen on the docks between fishermen. They must be very sharp knives that they use, he says. Do they always plunge them into the stomach? Sometimes two fishermen must gut each other when it's a draw. Have you seen something like that? He is always asking questions that he answers with his own stories but when we speak about where I sail my boat for the fish, he listens and then writes down what I tell him in a black book he bought in Paris.

He wants to know about the big fish. It's always the stories with big fish in them that he wants to hear. I tell him I live off the small fish. They are for food, and the big fish are for being a hero. They are for famous men like the Yankee and the free people in the homes of the brave over the waters. Boatfuls of people drown for stories like the Yankee tells about being brave and free and rich, but me and my wife just stay quiet most of the time.

Sometimes we talk about the people in the market and dockyards, sometimes our family, if something nice has happened to the nephews and nieces. Gabriella's cousin got a job as a teacher in Guantanamo. I tell her it's a lovely city because Gabriella has never been there. It is good for him to live there with his new wife and Santiago Junior, his beautiful baby boy. We are very proud of him becoming a teacher so we talk about Santiago, in bed, when it is quiet and dark and the Yankee has gone back to the hotel to drink cocktails and make love with women on the clean sheets in the air conditioning.

Gabriella says Santiago was a clever little boy. She remembers that when they were children together, her cousin liked the books with numbers and letters in them, and he said intelligent things but she can't remember what they were anymore, and so she makes the sounds of a starving dog again. I can say nothing because I have already drowned and I must remain quiet and can only move close to her head and breathe over her without touching the noise. I have learned this from the way the water talks. All we can do is let the winds and tides change the world. In the morning I wake and there is a note on the kitchen table from the Yankee that says he's got what he needs for his story and he won't be coming back. There is more money than we agreed, but the baby shoes from the wall are gone and I am worried what will happen when Gabriella sees what he stole from us.

the rattler
LIGHT
VEHIC
MAY TR
ON
TRAM TRACK

The Rattler

A BLAST OFF, OF SORTS

On Tuesday afternoon Atticus came home with a monster of leather and chrome. Big. Black. Brutal. Smelling of fine cigars. Rolling into place like it was set to take off at Cape Canaveral in T minus thirty seconds. He looked at the massive office chair behind his desk at home, and after a few silent moments of contemplation, said in a small voice, 'Fucken hell.'

His wife, April, asked him when she saw it that night, "What the hell did you do?" She blinked at it. "What have you done? You can't handle that. Look at your desk for God's sake. It looks like a scared Chihuahua about to be mounted by an angry Great Dane."

"Shhh." Atticus waved at her like she might get the chair angry. "Shoosh. Go away. I want to write."

His wife looked at him and then back at the monster office chair. The cash register bell struck in her brain.

"How much did that thing cost? We can't afford it. It must have cost an arm and a kidney. You know there's…"

"Yes, I know. I know! You don't need to tell me we can't afford it. I didn't buy it." Atticus and April looked at each other for a moment. "It just came my way," he told her.

"I'll check the credit card tomorrow. There's no point in lying."

"Check it now. I'm not lying."

"So… how?"

He didn't answer and they went on looking from the doorway at the monster office chair in his pokey little study. She growled low, "How?"

THE WHISTLING VIRTUOSO
AND THE SHOW DOGS

Atticus O'Neill had wanted to write a book for ages. It annoyed him when people talked about writing their life stories some day because it belittled his own intention to write his biography. Or when they said they'd retire and finally have a chance to write that great Australian novel. Atticus didn't go that far, but he daydreamed about writing the great book of Melbourne.

He could tell from the way people spoke that they thought there was something about their lives worth writing about. That wasn't true. Yet in his thirty odd years as a tram driver, Atticus had seen a few things. He had marvellous tales to tell but he found it impossible to sit at his desk for any length of time. He didn't have the patience, or it was a less tangible quality he lacked, but he found it difficult to approach the virgin white paper in his typewriter, teasing him with silent, defiant chastity. With his new office chair things were going to change.

He had a tram full of dogs once, thirteen years ago. They ran around the cabin trying to leap out the windows at cars driving past. Barking their heads off. Leaping onto each other and tussling. Some sat down on the seats and slid off when Atticus drew the tram to a stop. Some raised a leg and urinated when it was promised that they wouldn't. There were dogs with brightly coloured ribbons tied around their chests, others with red bows and blue bows on their heads, between their ears. A tiara on one. All on an emergency mission from a Dog Show to a primary school that had been burned to the ground. The devastated children were waiting in the gymnasium. The Dog Show's transport had broken down on the way. There was a story there... but how to tell it?

In his first years on the rails, Atticus worked with a whistler — a conductor who was a whistling virtuoso. It wasn't the kind of whistling that people found annoying. This was the kind that people wanted to hear, that amazed them and made them wonder why more people didn't do it. Why it wasn't an art form that you could see on a stage somewhere. People vowed to practise more around their homes.

This conductor had requests for certain tunes every day. In the mornings even the least patriotic got misty eyed over *Advance Australia Fair*. The medley of our national anthem, *Waltzing Matilda*, and Men at Work's *Down Under*, was a masterpiece. Commuters called him the Hendrix of the 96.

But Atticus couldn't find the words to describe the whistling that didn't make it sound trivial. He couldn't describe himself shedding a tear once because of a powerful late night whistled rendition of *Auld Lang Syne* as they moved along the Esplanade past the Espy Hotel, no-one but themselves and the lonely, empty embrace of Port Philip Bay reaching out for an ever aloof Apple Isle. It sounded silly when he put it to paper, but it hadn't been silly when he heard that conductor whistle. It still had the power to bring on misty eyes when Atticus thought about it and the altogether more humane days of the W-Class trams. Those festive, open-air Melbourne rattlers.

There was a driver called Chuck Denning. He'd always say someone 'axed' him a question, even after Atticus had pointed out the correct pronunciation. It was like a speech impediment. He never said, 'I'm going on a meal break', he'd say, 'I'm going on a mule break.' Atticus couldn't point out the error again, because even after ten years of swapping trams, Chuck Denning had never forgiven Atticus for the correction on ask/axe. And there was a story, a character at least, in there as well, wasn't there?

Atticus's problem was that he couldn't make the sentences roll. When he sat down to write about his father, he began, 'My father was a man of few words…' but where could he go from there? His father was so taciturn in Atticus's memories all he could do was imagine Atticus Senior peering grimly over his shoulder, shaking his head at this foolishness. *Get serious, Junior. Stop wasting time. Get back to your trams.*

A BIT OF A WANKER… BUT HAMLESS

It was shortly after acquiring the monster office chair that Atticus took a forced retirement. For weeks his wife thought it was a regular retirement. Eventually there was no hiding the fact that Atticus had done something very strange and had been fired for it.

"It's that bloody chair! It's given you ideas," April said.

"I've always had ideas," he murmured when she was out of earshot.

Atticus was doing the 96 yet again, and on the stretch of the route that took him around onto Fitzroy Street he realised the tram was completely empty. It was nine-thirty in the morning and there should have been at least one of the disgusting, smelly homeless taking their daily free cruise around the neighbourhood. Should have been at least an angry junkie couple swearing at each other about a further betrayal of an already taxed relationship. Should have been a few wagging students. Perhaps a prima donna beauty queen kissing words into her mobile as she applied a touch up of lip liner. Should have been a fat middle-aged geek daydreaming about the wisdom of getting an unobtrusive lightning bolt tattooed on his forehead with a Warhammer book and a t-shirt proclaiming undying love for Harry Potter.

Could have been one of those or any of the anonymous faces that didn't even make it into Atticus's book of human clichés. But there was no-one. He rolled on down Fitzroy with a clean, quiet, empty tram. When he got down to the Junction of Acland and Carlisle he had to wait a few minutes for the tram in the cul-de-sac to clear before he could proceed. It gave him a few moments to have a lovely literary reverie.

There was a fierce knocking on his door. A commuter wearing a matching powder-blue tracksuit continued to knock even though he could see Atticus looking at him through the glass doors. The commuter wanted to be taken down to Barkly Street. Atticus told him through the glass that it was a five minute walk; maybe less. That it'd be over ten minutes before the tram got down the end, to Barkly. The customer nodded as though he was saying, *Yeah, yeah, stop with the blabbering,* and made a winding gesture with his arm as if to say *Open the fuck up already, dickhead.* Atticus didn't open the door. He ignored the persistent knocking; even when it turned into kicking.

When he got down to the end of Acland he didn't open his doors. People knocked, but he didn't release the doors. He looked up the street at the madness of pedestrians crossing at will, weaving through all the restless cars, coffee drinkers bearing the precious brew within lifted paper cups, ruthless taxis and bustling bikes and fish trucks and one fool towing a trailer with nothing but a tall fridge barely strapped down. All of this amid the autumn sunshine that seemed so bright and sharp it was as though the frame of the sky had broken and was raining down glass in billions of fragments. And there they were, banging on the doors to be let in, to be transported through it all to their unknowable private destinations and destinies.

Chuck Denning was coming down Acland and would refuse to acknowledge him again, even if Atticus waved a friendly finger at him. Atticus put the tram in drive and let it coast up Acland, pushed the bell to ring out a warning as he passed Denning, and then gave him the bird. When that didn't seem enough he brought up his other arm and gave him a double bird. In his imagination he was like one of those Hippy gods bringing out a hundred hands each bearing the finger for Chuck.

That wasn't why Atticus got fired. Chuck Denning never mentioned it to the supervisors and investigators when they came around and asked about the day Atticus went off the rails. Denning's only comment, repeated ten different ways, was that Atticus was alright. A bit of a wanker… but hamless.

BARBETTE OF BROADMEADOWS

April told Atticus her daughter was coming to stay. "Barbette's bringing the baby. I don't want you to worry. Dylan's an angel. And it's only going to be for a week or two."

When Atticus explained that he'd just freed himself from the drudgery of labour for his life long dream of literary liberation and pointed out that an unhappy mother and her bawling baby kind of defeated the purpose, she deployed an argument aggravated and aggrieved in sliding and shifting particulars.

Economics and familial bonds were chief points for which Atticus could find no adequate rebuttal or recourse. To argue made him seem like a heartless arsehole.

April went on to say that Barbette was distressed that her relationship with Richard had dissolved so soon after Dylan was born. He could barely be called a baby. An infant. Barbette would have to go back to work, though the kind of work she did wasn't going to be easy to find, even in a bohemian area like Elwood. Reiki might have made her some money, but she practised a kind of massage where she didn't actually touch the person she was performing the massage on. She cleansed their aura.

Before Barbette, the phone had barely rung. If it did, it was an even money chance that the voice on the other end of the line would be Indian accented. Now it was better odds it would be Dylan's daddy.

Richard was an organic baker who set up a store in Broadmeadows despite being assured that Health Food in that area wasn't a booming business. But Richard was an egalitarian. He gave away a lot of wood-fired oven organic bread. He planted trees in local parks. He said good morning and good evening like a one-man force for the resurrection of polite social values. He got beaten up by local toughs and shrugged off the bruises. Along with his yoga classes, Richard started taking kick-boxing classes.

Barbette couldn't stand living in Broadmeadows and had to get out of there. Richard came over to persuade Barbette to come back to him and the bakery. But she would never be 'Barbette of Broadmeadows,' no matter how great a title that would make for a story Atticus might write.

April said, "It's only for a few days."

Barbette said, "It's only going to be for a few weeks."

Dylan spent much of his time wailing and bawling into eternity.

At first, Atticus was interested in how it would all turn out. But the weeks moved on. She was now permanently installed in the lounge. It became less interesting as a story. 'Barb and Dyl of the sitting room, now impromptu nursery' wasn't a good story. Not at all. It was hard on Atticus who never had children of his own.

His previous wife, Glenda, didn't like children, and Atticus hadn't loved children enough to press the issue. He didn't know what to do with Dylan when Barbette went out to give one of her massages.

The only thing he wanted to write about was the incredible hair Dylan had, but that would be weird. Still, there it was, every day. The baby couldn't speak a sensible word but he had a rich lustrous mane of flowing hair that reminded Atticus of Hollywood starlets. Every time he looked at the kid it disturbed him. Maybe it had something to do with sparkling cleansed auras and organic obsessed breast milk.

THE ROGUE TRAM

Atticus didn't think of himself as gay but when he went to the hairdresser he wasn't sure. You couldn't switch for the other side as late as your fifties could you, he wondered. But he looked forward to Christian massaging his scalp when he was preparing him for a haircut. April complained about the cost of the boutique cut but it was a luxury he didn't want to sacrifice. The smells alone were worth the price of admission. Everything aromatic of renewal. If renaissance had a smell, it was surely this.

His own hair was nothing like the lush blessing little Dylan could boast of. No, poor old Atticus had a more hardy type of crop growing on the top paddock. It was grey and black and white; the texture of wire. Pig hair, he called it, but maybe he was being unkind to himself. Men his age often got bristly hair. There was nothing about a bit of scalp showing through to be ashamed of either.

He used to go to a local men's cutter, a Russian called Yuri, who smelled of bitter coffee and tobacco and loved nothing better than to talk about women with big breasts. He even brought out photos of women with cow udders jutting from their chests. Cut from magazines and glued to a scrap book of mammary glory. Ten dollars for a cut from Yuri but it always made Atticus feel queasy when Yuri came close enough to breathe on his neck. What was an extra forty dollars if you could go in and get Christian and his powerful fingers massaging your scalp?

Atticus closed his eyes and groaned.

Afterwards, he was escorted by a pretty young girl who asked him if he wanted tea or coffee, and he always said yes please to a coffee. But this'd have to be the last time, since he hadn't been working for months. He didn't know how he was going to break it to Christian.

Unaware of the impending end to their relationship, Christian left a good-natured hand on Atticus's shoulder and asked him, "So how's the writing going?"

"Oh well... I've had a few ideas." Atticus moved from sulky demurral to bright optimism in the space of those seven words. It had a lot to do with the great listener he had in Christian. Usually... today Christian was distracted and overly talkative.

"Well, I've got a story for you, mate," he told Atticus. "And apparently it's true. It's about a rogue tram driver." Christian paused in his preparation and looked at Atticus. "You haven't already heard this?" Atticus didn't move his head. He looked ahead at the images in the mirror as though it was a large windscreen he'd been staring through for decades.

The hairdresser continued, "A tram driver drove every route in the city, all day long, without opening his doors. I mean this guy had lost his shit and just drove on everywhere until they had to box him in, force him out of his tram, raving. *The Rogue Tram Driver.* That's a title for you." Having said all that he still wasn't paying attention to Atticus. He was busy running a comb through a few wisps of his hair instead.

Atticus murmured, "Raving… grumbling maybe… what raving… do people even know raving from murmuring…?"

Christian leaned forward to try to catch the murmured words. "What's that Mister Atticus?" A lovely smile crossed his face like summer sunshine across a blue sky. Atticus said he needed a glass of water and the spritely Christian went off to get it for him rather than ask an assistant. He came back and placed it before Atticus with another one of those summer-sweet smiles.

Atticus asked, "What do you think about Yuri around the corner? Are you offended by his very presence? A hack hairdresser like that? You must laugh at him and the men that go in there for their ten dollar haircuts."

The girl, Reagan, slid into Christian's shadow to tell him his wife was on the phone. His wife Josephine was already over nine months pregnant. Updates coming in, on the hour. She was experiencing cramps.

"I think Yuri is charging twenty bucks now," Christian said flatly. "Just give me a second Mister Atticus." It was always the joking 'Mister.' Atticus called him Mister Christian in return. He'd miss that. With Yuri, there wasn't even a hello. It was just a nod at one of the two chairs and a murmured 'Sit'. Or, 'Wait.'

When Christian came back from his phone call it was impossible to ask him again what he thought of Yuri without giving his hand away. That he and Yuri would in fact be sharing mammarical intimacies from now on. Was it true that Yuri had a wife back in Russia with ten children as well as the wife he had in Australia with five? That he also had a mistress? That he hired the occasional apprentice to have yet more sexual adventures with? That's what Yuri said but who knew if you could believe a word? Perhaps he had no mistresses or extra wives at all and at home he took out the garbage obediently when Katerina told him to.

Atticus' hairdresser might have answers to these questions but instead he heard Christian say, "On Tuesday they're going to induce Josephine."

Atticus said, "Wow." Frowned at himself in the mirror. "Tuesday hey? So you're a dad by this time next week. Should I congratulate you now?"

"Better not jinx it."

"I love that word. Why don't we use it more often?"

"Which?"

"Jinx." Atticus unfrowned his face. He liked being draped in the black sheet that protected his clothes from his wiry hair. He entertained the idea of a character who begins to wear a black cape to work. Who changes his name to Jinx. He could be an oncologist. His eccentricities were of the Robin Williams sort and people could be healed or at least die with a smile on their faces.

"You could use it for a name… if it didn't have such negative connotations. It sounds good though, doesn't it? Jinx."

"Yeah," Christian said distractedly. His wife being induced didn't come as a relief. She'd been resisting the idea. Didn't want to consider a Caesarean even though the doctor was telling her the baby was a whale calf.

Atticus was annoyed that Christian was being so closed mouthed and distracted now. Their last haircut together. "Say it. Try it out. Jinx."

Christian stopped cutting. His blue eyes blinked and a cloud passed across his clear, fresh as the morning face. "What… Jinx?"

"Doesn't that sound pretty in your mouth. Say it again."

"Jinx." Christian started cutting again. "But as you say. It's not the kind of name you give a kid." Christian trimmed around the back of Atticus's head.

"Well, it's a shame," Atticus said. There was a silence in which he had time to reflect that Christian would never again bring his expert hands near Atticus' face. He asked, "Hey, do you remember the first time I came in here?"

Christian guffawed. He stepped back to wipe the smile from his face. It was a greasy grin and so unlike the pleasing Christian, Atticus thought.

"The rat's tail." Christian said, his big, luminescent teeth glittering like a corrupted angel. "I still have it out back. That long grey thing."

"It was a ponytail," Atticus corrected him. He looked at the young blonde who was a mockery of everything outside glossy fashion magazines, and was furious. This wasn't how it was supposed to go. Their last time together. All Christian cared about today was his pregnant wife. Like millions of women hadn't already popped out hundreds of billions of children already. "Say it," he said.

"Say what?"

"It wasn't a rat's tail. Say ponytail."

Christian opened and closed his scissors mid-air.

"Are you kidding?"

"No." Atticus watched the hairdresser shift from one foot to the other. "Say ponytail."

Again Christian worked his scissors mid-air. "...Ponytail."

They didn't talk again until it was time to pay, and even then there was no Mister Atticus or Mister Christian. There wasn't even the standard request to schedule their next hair cut in six weeks. Atticus asked Christian to go out back and bring him the ponytail. It came out in a plastic envelope, like a zoological specimen.

A MORE VERSATILE MIRROR

Atticus wanted April to parrot phrases or words like Christian.

"You might have a big shot chair now, but it doesn't mean I'm taking dictation. You should be taking out the rubbish. It's overflowing. Can you take it out now?"

"You want me to take out the rubbish?" He looked at her with a flat, hard expression on his face. "You want me to take out the rubbish?" If he couldn't get her to repeat what he told her to say, he could turn it around and repeat what she was saying. He laid stress on odd bits of the sentence as he repeated it yet again. "You want me to take out the rubbish?" In his own mind he was deconstructing all the parts of what April was trying to say to him. Getting her to look at the brutal imposition of her string of words as she interrupted his time with the blank page.

He'd been developing an idea of the page as a kind of mirror that one had to stare into for long enough, and only then would it yield up its reflections. He was prepared to wait for days, for weeks, for months and years. But eventually the page would come alive. All he needed was enough time to stare into the snow-white surface of his pristine white paper.

"You heard me," she said. "You suddenly become deaf or stupid—or both? For God's sake, take, the, rubbish, out. Please!" She did some fake sign language at him, which usually would have made him laugh.

Not this time.

She waited at his office doorway for him to leave his chair. He would only do it reluctantly because once out of it, he knew it wouldn't be that easy to get back into it. April would find other things for him to do. There was a bath rail to be reattached to the wall. There were dishes she'd want assistance with. And then there'd be dinner to help her prepare. There was just no way for him to devote enough time to the office chair and the paper before it. The hours he'd spent searching its spaces would be wasted.

He repeated her sentence one more time. Added her 'please' at the end of it, and slowly swung around to face the window so all she saw was the back of the malevolent monster office chair. Atticus heard the shuffle of her slippers across the carpet as she mumbled out into another room. Almost unheard of for April to give up like that.

THE ONE ESSENTIAL MESSAGE

Atticus was in his chair, pushing the buttons of his typewriter, one by one. He moved letter to letter rather than word to word. He was feeling so despondent about breaking up with Christian all he could write was poetry. He wanted to write a haiku but he couldn't remember how many syllables were supposed to go on each line. He wrote: Corrupted Angel. Cut out my liver. Feed it to your dog. Letter by letter, he had changed some of the words many times. Liver changed from heart to soul, brain, ears, eyes, liver, kidneys and back to liver again. And the dog had been a crow, a vulture, and a baby, but that seemed perverse, so he was now typing j-a-c-k-a-l.

"I'm no expert, but that doesn't sound like writing to me," said April.

"What do you mean?" Atticus jerked the paper from his typewriter and screwed it up into a ball.

"It should sound like the rain falling on a tin roof. Words pouring onto the page."

"Maybe I need a rain doctor," he said.

"Well, some kind of doctor," she said.

His friend David Dickens came over a few days later. Atticus had told April to tell David he wasn't home if he happened to call but April had asked David to come and talk with Atticus.

He was seated across the desk from Atticus. Atticus did half turns left and right as he contemplated what David Dickens was telling him.

David had become interested in graffiti. He considered it a spontaneous social phenomenon that reached back beyond the graffiti-ridden walls of Rome to the caves themselves. He had been examining a series of messages that appeared around a hospital out in Sandringham.

"You wouldn't believe the continuity I've found in these erratic messages, and the subtle contrasts of the one essential message."

"The One Essential Message," repeated Atticus as he swivelled left and right in his monster office chair. His head moved but his eyes remained fixed on the man across the desk.

An odd expression crossed David's face, but he continued, "I exist. I'm here."

"This is the rationale for you cruising late night train stations? Going to this hospital to investigate graffiti? This is how you spend your time? This is why you gave up your work at the clinic?" On the other side of the table his hippie psychologist friend looked somewhat small and foolish, though David was over six foot tall.

He was taller than Atticus but David was sitting on an old kitchen chair. It was the wooden chair Atticus used to have behind his small desk, and it was now deployed as a visitor's chair, to downsize the hippie. David had written a book. Not a proper book. Just some non-fiction essay type thing printed with no fanfare by a publisher barely anyone had ever heard of in South Australia. It was nothing like the towering monument to literature that Atticus would write someday. Someday soon.

"Who wants to think about graffiti?" Atticus asked.

David looked at his old friend. Atticus still swivelling with menace, right and left in his immense new office chair. David squeezed his face into a puckered expression, opened back out into a bemused smile again and wobbled his head. He'd picked up that head wobble from his constant travelling to India for yoga and spiritual insight, where he bought his shirts patterned with elephants, and pants that looked like they were made from gaudy handkerchiefs. It looked about as genuine as young Australian suburbanites striking homeboy poses dressed in their latest hip-hop gear in local shopping malls.

"Well, me for one. I find it interesting that we have our youth going out there in the dead of night, risking their lives along those rails, climbing over fences and reaching up to precarious places, so that they can carve intricate social messages to the general population come the light of day. And that this has been going on, uninterrupted all the way back through to the Neanderthal's handprint against a rock."

"Neanderthals and Vandals. Juvenile delinquents. Bored suburban kids using a texta to write their names on a clean carriage wall. Why would anyone care about these things?"

"Well, I don't know."

David's head wobbled again.

"Well, I don't know." Atticus echoed the words.

The two old friends didn't have much more to say after that. David left the room, wobbling his head at April, while Atticus turned his seat to the window and began to gaze out into the dirty, grey wool strewn out across the Melbourne sky. On the window sill sat a god with the head of an elephant. Ganesha. That's the name

David gave this silly creature when he brought it back with him on his last trip. Atticus hadn't thrown it away because he had an idea for a story. He'd even written the first sentence. "One day Greg Samuels woke up and found that he had the head of an elephant." There was a nod at Kafka of course, but he thought, wouldn't it be interesting if everyone in the world suddenly had the heads of different animals. But what then? What would the head of an elephant feel like? He looked at Ganesha and felt enervated by his apparent goodwill.

Atticus soon discovered that just a few months earlier an Australian writer called Hawthorne Hardachre had come out with just that idea. It made Atticus feel a furious kind of vindication. A novel peopled with characters who had the heads of Egyptian gods isn't how Atticus would have done it, but there was the essential idea. Valid as all hell and a popular success to boot. Journalists were predicting awards.

He stuck a clean blank page into his typewriter and typed the title of his great novel: The One Essential Message. There was a character who would be covered in graffiti from head to toe. He was tattooed with the words spoken all around him. The accretion of the thousands of people speaking through him all the way back into childhood. It was a disease that manifested the words spoken at him.

Atticus was excited. He asked himself what if it was the other way around and everyone in the world was covered in graffiti, tattooed all the way up and down, and it was as normal as tans and turbans in India, but there was one man alone in the world sitting in a bus shelter, waiting, who had clean clear blank skin. Somehow he hadn't been overwritten with everyone else's voices and words and thoughts and ideas. Yes, a clear image to start the book. A man sitting in a bus shelter, a blank face. Maybe an airport terminal. Waiting. About to go somewhere.

First Atticus was going to need a tea though, so he got up and put a pot on. Maybe a few biscuits as well.

GOD WILL SORT A FEW THINGS OUT

"What's the time?"

Atticus was standing in the Writing Reference section in the bookstore. Atticus already had every book on the shelf worth owning. Not that he'd read every one of those at home, but he'd started them all and had an idea of what they all contained. That imparted an immense feeling of poised potential. Lately he'd been sitting in his office chair and cradling one or two of the books, flipping through the pages. It was the grand possibility embedded in life that he was looking for. There was a feeling of potency that a book on metaphors could give him. Or a weighty book of symbols. And maybe it was the reason he came to this section of the bookstore so often. Looking for another way through.

"I asked you a question. What's the time?"

Atticus had just looked at his watch when the man standing next to him noticed.

"Excuse me," Atticus said, picking up the wonderful Paris Review Interviews he bought a few weeks ago. Volume Three. The Martin Amis interview was exceptional. But he was picking it up now so that he wouldn't have to be empty handed as he tried to dismiss this interloper.

"What's the time?"

"I don't want to talk to you. That should be clear to even the most obtuse."

"What?" The man took a breath and then a step back to face the diminutive Atticus. "What's the time, for fuck's sake. That's all I'm asking you. I don't want a conversation. Just the time. I saw you check your watch. You don't even need to bend your elbow again."

"I don't appreciate your tone." Atticus hadn't looked at the man next to him, but could see from the corner of his eye that he was swivelling his head left and right angrily, as though looking for a witness to this outrage. But Atticus went on, "Am I an automaton for you to use for the time?"

"A what?" The interloper didn't know what automaton meant, and clearly he didn't even belong in the Writing Reference area. "The time, fuckhead! What's the fucking time? Simple question! Simple answer!"

"It's Sunday afternoon. Why would you need the precise time?"

"What the fuck is this? Someone asks you for the time and you want justification? You want reasons and explanations? Just give me the time, you wanker."

A woman with children, looking at books in the nearby Children's area, came over and said, "It's just after three-thirty. Is there a reason to argue like this in front of children?"

"You see. How hard was that?" asked the man. "What a drop-kick," he said to the children with an embarrassed smile and shake of his head as he walked away.

It left Atticus alone in the Reference area, which was the way he preferred it. Atticus wasn't wrong either, though it would have saved him the aggravation if he'd just given the rude man the time. There were subtle social conventions that people had forgotten. Atticus would have been more than willing to give the man the time had he said 'Excuse me.' But Atticus had been asked a million times, *Does this tram go to the city? Does this tram go down Bourke Street? When will this tram get to Chapel Street? How would I get to Prospect Street, Box Hill?* A hundred million times. It was countless. Numberless like passing street lights

132

night after night on the same route for ten years straight. Like raindrops running across the broad windscreen of a tram. Like commuters entering and leaving the cabin never saying hello or good-bye. Those questions asked without an 'Excuse Me,' or a 'Thank-You.' A kind of brutal *Hey, Mr. Automaton, keep driving the tram, just shut the fuck up, and tell me what I need to know.* Atticus wasn't insane. That was there in the tone of their voices. They knew it and he knew it. He'd reached a point where he was unable to ignore it.

Atticus continued to look through the Writing Reference area and was excited to discover a book he'd never seen before on writing dialogue for scripts. He hadn't written much dialogue before and many of the books said he should.

He took the book to the counter and paid for it. He felt offended by the t-shirt of the sales assistant. Also by the fact that he wasn't greeted or given a good-bye. That the sales assistant went on with a conversation he was having with another sales assistant. His t-shirt had a skull on it wearing a green military beret surrounded by the words *Kill'em all, and let God sort'em out.*

Atticus had walked outside but he stepped into the bookstore again and went back to the counter and raised his wrist as he consulted his watch.

"It's now three forty seven in the afternoon." And waited for a reaction.

The sales assistant with the Marines t-shirt just nodded dumbly.

But Atticus didn't move and looked at his watch again. "It's now three forty eight in the afternoon," he stated.

The sales assistants looked at each other and the one with the t-shirt said, "Thank-you...?"

Atticus said, "You make me want to put a stink on my fist."

He didn't know what it meant but he'd heard a commuter say that. Atticus knew the Marine t-shirt would understand what it meant.

A VERY STRANGE SOUND

The phone was ringing. Atticus roused himself from a nap in his accommodating office chair. It had a head rest and its all leather upholstery was moulded to his back, and the arm rests were long and scalloped so that he could rest each arm from elbow to wrist within them. His legs were on the desk and he was as comfy as he would have been in bed.

The phone was still ringing. He opened his thick lips like a retarded frog getting its mouth working. He pulled his heavy legs off the desk. Thought about letting the phone ring out, but swallowed and climbed out of his office chair. Got to the phone by about the twentieth ring.

"Mmmello," he murmured.

"Ah yes, I wanted to speak to April."

Atticus took his time. "Is that the way you say hello?"

"Yes. What?" The voice didn't speak for a moment. "Hello?" This time the kind that asks what the hell was going on.

"I think you need a little more practise. And again. This time like you mean it."

"Hell-lo," he said, now mocking Atticus.

"Amazing. They must have been teaching you that word since you were a child, and you would think you'd have it by now. Still can't say it without insulting the whole idea of greeting someone and asking them for a moment of their time. As if you weren't pulling someone from the urgency of their own lives with the pointless interruption of your own inane questions."

The voice didn't say anything. Atticus was about to hang up

but could hear the caller breathing on the other end of the line and he was curious as to how he might possibly respond to that.

Eventually the voice said, "Fair point actually." After another moment of consideration, the caller said, "Well, now I suppose a greeting would be a bit redundant. If I could take just another moment of your time, I'll get to my reason for calling. I wanted to speak to April but perhaps I can speak to you regarding the sale of an office chair. I'd like to come over and have a look at it. It seems a great deal at fifty dollars. Maybe too good to be true though, so I would like to see it. I live around the corner. I could be there in fifteen minutes. If it's as described, I'll take it off your hands."

Atticus could hear the man on the other end of the line, breathing. Waiting. Ready to come right over and take the office chair away, still warm from Atticus' nap.

"Sir? Those gargling noises don't sound good. Are you all right?" The voice on the other end of the line sounded genuinely concerned. "I mean, it sounds like you're choking. Should I call the ambulance?" The voice called out to someone named Linda, telling her about an emergency. "Oh my God — what's going on over there? Can you just tell me your address. That's the most terrible sound I've heard in my life. Sir? Sir? Please let me know how to help you…"

Atticus hung up the phone. He walked back to his study slowly. Dylan had been woken by the very strange sound Atticus made while on the phone and was now crying. Atticus stood in his doorway and looked at the monster office chair behind his little desk. It was like someone had given him the terrible news that a loved one had a terminal disease. Only a few months to live so that when you looked at them they seemed to already be disappearing. That's how he felt looking at the office chair of leather and chrome he'd brought home not so long ago.

Big. Black. Brutal. Smelling of fine cigars. So full of power and potential. A promise of a ride to anywhere you could dream of going—fading before his eyes.

DEATH BY A THOUSAND BUTS

Barbette had decided she wanted to give acting a go. People had always told her she had a theatrical streak. That she had a natural grace when she moved. She could shed tears at will and she loved watching films. She even went by herself to the cinema when she couldn't get a friend to go along with her. She watched television shows and believed in the HBO revolution like some in previous generations had believed in democracy and the USA. Barbette knew she could leap tall buildings if someone helped her with the truth and justice parts.

A few months after Barbette had installed herself in the lounge, she'd had a terrible nightmare. She was being chased down a street by a group of men and their dogs. They were relentless in their hunt. They were dressed in the red hunting gear of Old England but it was through industrial urban landscapes that they followed her.

Dream Barbette ran through crowds but no-one noticed her danger. Exhausted, she ran into a building and stumbled past hundreds of people dressed in Aussie Rules scarves and beanies, discreetly seated in a vast, elegant theatre, watching a play. Dream Barbette knew the men in red and their howling hounds would erupt into the theatre and she would have nowhere to hide, so she raced up onto the stage to find an exit in the wings, but before she could, she was captured by someone on stage. When she started screaming, others rushed onto stage to assist her. But she realised these actors were including her in the play. What's more, the hunters and their dogs had settled into the audience and were watching.

　　　　　　　　　　　The Rattler & other stories

Dream Barbette began to enjoy being an actor but knew that as soon as the performance finished she'd be revealed for who she was and they would swoop on her. She woke drenched in sweat, shaking with fear and exhilaration. She went on to call this her Damascus dream.

It'd been half a year already that Barbette and Dylan had been camped out in the lounge. It looked as though that was going to go on. Every time Atticus approached April regarding her daughter and grandson, there was an argument.

"In the first place, my daughter has nowhere else to go." April said ticking off the points on her fingers by raising a thumb. "Two," raising a forefinger, "Dylan can't be kicked to the curb."

She didn't tick any more points off, but that half fist of unfolded fingers stayed before his eyes like a threat. Within April's fist was Atticus and his new career as a writer and there was his ongoing unemployment. He wasn't sure what else she had in that unfurled hand but there were probably more points than fingers.

A cheap motel was a suggestion Atticus wouldn't dare voice. "A flat somewhere?"

"Are you kidding? Have you seen what those blood suckers are charging for rent these days? Atticus, come on, where's your heart?" April asked.

April looked at him like he was a monster just for bringing it up. And there was the rent that Barbette paid. There was just no discussing it. So Atticus stayed in his study and felt guilty about taking up a room that could be used to improve baby Dylan's living situation. Barbette converted the sun room into a nice little bedroom, draped everywhere with colourful fabrics. It reminded Atticus of Jeannie's room in her bottle on the show *I Dream of Jeannie.*

Besides, he was getting used to it. Barbette was getting so comfortable in her new home, half the time she walked around in little more than underwear. Sometimes even less. She was still breast feeding Dylan and was enjoying the generous breasts she now had. Went on about how otherwise no-one would ever be able to tell she'd ever even had a baby. Of course Atticus reacted as a full grown man would, but he also found it more and more annoying that Barbette seemed oblivious to that fact.

Atticus sat in his room reading. If he wasn't reading he went on sitting in his office chair brooding. Barbette crossed to and fro, past his open door. She wanted to tell him she'd be going to get some milk, or some bread, that there was a letter for him, that she was going to have a shower and perhaps he could look after Dylan, and lately she was bringing scripts in.

Atticus had never looked at scripts before. He'd never even read a play outside of Romeo and Juliet and Hamlet at school. He wanted to get back to his white paper musing, his story and memoir contemplations, but it looked like he was doing nothing when Barbette came into his study and it was hard to argue against her in all her half-naked enthusiasm. Initially all she wanted him to do was read parts with her, but she soon started asking Atticus what he thought about certain passages. About the various motivations of characters.

"But what does she want?" Barbette asked as she breastfed Dylan.

Atticus said, "Motivation is mostly about what we don't want. In her case, ask yourself what she's running away from."

And they'd launch into another round of reading screenplays. Scripts like *Tender Mercies* by Horton Foote caught Atticus's imagination. He'd never even seen the film and was surprised to find out it was directed by an Australian. He watched it and loved it even more—could have continued to go over the lines with Barbette happily, but she brought in other screenplays for them to work on. Richard had begun to come for Dylan every day so they had a lot of time. She got dressed when Richard came around.

Atticus began to write in earnest. He'd never really thought about scripts or screenplays, but he really liked working with dialogue. It was so easy it barely seemed like work. He didn't have to worry about descriptive details which had killed the whole process of writing for him. He didn't have to worry about anything but what people were doing and saying. And he could see all that very clearly.

Barbette was a hairdresser called Harriet just opening up a salon in Elwood. There was a nearby men's salon run by a man called Ivan. A leering, bald Bulgarian who kept coming over, ostensibly to give her advice about running a hairdressers because he'd been in operation for twenty years.

The characters that came into the salon all had interesting stories to tell, and this in itself was perfect for the kinds of vignettes Atticus had stored in his mind for the last thirty years.

Harriet the Hairdresser had an angry mechanic husband who kept storming into the salon demanding Harriet come back to him. He threatened to steal back young baby Joshua. The infant had Dylan's long, thick, luxurious hair.

Atticus could see it was a formless mishmash of events and people. That it wasn't decided yet on being the tragedy of a vulnerable young woman trying to nurse her baby while running a new business, surrounded by destructive male presences like Ivan the Bulgarian Cutter and Michael the Mechanic, or on being just a comedy about the folly of desires and ambitions. He knew his depiction of women was stereotypical, that Harriet didn't ever really become anything but a foil for the lusts and wills around her.

Atticus was thrilled to be writing. In fact, he was writing a lot. In only four weeks he'd completed the first draft of a screenplay called *Death By A Thousand Cuts*. At the end of those one hundred and twenty pages (a figure decided upon by Syd Field in his bible of screen writing, *Screenplay* – a reference book Atticus read, start to finish) Atticus had created something complete and whole.

One hundred and twenty pages. However good or bad it was, there was a beginning, middle and end. And it could be filmed tomorrow. Everything that a film needed to be made from a script was there in the pile of paper called, *Death By A Thousand Cuts*. Below that title were the words, by A. S. O'Neill.

Barbette and Atticus had performed some of it, but just before it was fully polished, Barbette suddenly asked Richard to take Dylan and left for a new acting academy out in Warrnambool. She'd be gone for months.

It left Atticus with a pile of papers and it didn't matter what it was called. He couldn't send it out to anyone because what producer wanted to read a screenplay from someone who'd never acted, directed, even catered for a film?

Who wanted to read a script written by an ex-tram driver about the troubled lives of hysterical hairdressers in Elwood?

THE GARDEN GNOME

"I've got you a job, honey."

"What?" Atticus was so stunned that he couldn't put the right kind of acid into the question. It should have been the most corrosive vitriol—not a meek question.

April just opened her mouth like a happy frog plucking flies out of juicy swamp air. "You'll love it, Atty. Driving a taxi."

The phone rang before Atticus could go mental at his frog wife and her mouth full of flies. April answered on the first ring.

It was Richard on the other end of the line. "Oh, hey Dicky. How's things?" Without waiting for Richard to reply, April continued, "We're pretty good over here. Great in fact. Barbette's doing well. Things are starting to happen you know, but let me tell you about the great job I found Atty."

"I'm not driving a fucking taxi," Atticus said.

"Of course he's been writing up a storm but we can all use inspiration, and what better inspiration than people—every one of them with a story. You know how it is? Everybody loves talking to taxi drivers."

"No taxi!" Atticus said.

"At his age, you've got to keep moving. On the move, you know. This whole state used to be about that. *Victoria on the Move.* Because my man's a garden gnome. If I leave him in one spot in the morning, there he is when I get home again. My beautiful little garden gnome."

"I'm fucking not driving a fucking taxi. You fucken hear me, woman? Fuck! I'm trying to write here."

He didn't usually like swearing as much as that but he couldn't seem to get the message across.

Speaking into the phone, with her eyes closed now, April said, "Atty's saying he won't drive a taxi. You know how he is, though. Coming around to sense via a stubborn thicket of stupidity. But he always gets there in the end."

Atticus was vibrating with off-white anger. Here he was sitting at his desk. In his monster office chair, actually writing, and his wife was an impudent frog leaping onto the typewriter before him, so that all his words and everything he'd written today swarmed up into the air like black gnat-like bits of useless fury. If he had a gun handy he would have picked it up and put a bullet either through his own head or April's, but he looked around and there was nothing even vaguely weapon-like. Just a stapler. And April was taking the cordless phone out of the study to talk about the wonderful world of taxi driving with the Baker of Broadmeadows.

"Well, she got a show already you know. A big one. It's going to tour the nation." A pause as April listened to Richard ask a question. "Well, you wouldn't believe it. Maybe I should let her tell you, because she swore me to secrecy, but I'm so excited. A musical. A song and dance number. They'll even be touring the UK. *Neighbours - The Musical*. She's going to be Daphne. You remember. She was a stripper, and that's how she met the guy with the big ears she marries on Ramsay Street. What was his name?"

"His name was Des," murmured Atticus.

He swivelled around in his office chair and contemplated the view of Elwood canal outside his window. A man walked along, slowing to read the chalk drawings that had recently been scrawled onto the path by some of the neighbourhood's children, but he didn't pause. He carried a colourful umbrella above his head, though it had stopped raining half an hour ago. Ducks were dropping from the sky, coming in for fancy skidding landings on the water. An old man was out there throwing bread crumbs like he did every afternoon. The sunlight was beginning to fade from the sky above the canal ducks and their benefactor. The lights in Atticus's pokey study were beginning to turn the window into a black mirror.

"I'm not driving a fucken taxi," he said again, trying to convince the malevolent reflection swivelling left and right in the window.

PITY FOR THE W-CLASS

The knock on the door couldn't be for Atticus so he went to answer it full of resentment for being dislodged from his study.

He was working on an interesting story in his head and he'd been pondering its significance.

The protagonist owned a small business. A little store that had been converted, from an old tailor he'd known in Port Melbourne who'd died of Creutzfeldt-Jacob disease ten years ago. A disease that hit like Alzheimer's times ten and killed him in a few weeks. Marie, the old Tailor's wife, had told Atticus at the funeral that statistically it was literally a one in a million disease. She kept saying that to everyone as though she wanted to convert the trivia of it into something more useful or profound.

Atticus was going to use some details in his story. He would have a character buy the old Tailor's store in Port Melbourne. It would begin with the new owner painting the walls again and again, looking to create a white surface, as pristine as a sheet of A4. He polished the floor boards. Made sure the old Tailor's two rooms of business were as empty as a place could possibly be. The large front window was perfectly clean. He put small tables into the room with one chair at each table and he was ready to open to the public. He put a sign on the window with his hours of operation.

The strange thing was, this was as far as the story went. People would come into the room and sit at a table. They would ask for nothing and he wouldn't give them anything but a place to sit. The story ends with him flipping the sign to say he was open and then stepping back to see who would come in.

Atticus was thinking it would be reminiscent of *The Ballad of the Sad Café* by Carson McCullers, but it'd been too long since he read that novella. So he was picking it off his shelf when the knock at the door disrupted him.

There was another brutal rap on the door, making him jump as he reached out for the handle. He opened the door ready to release a torrent of verbal violence but shut his mouth and blinked when he saw who it was.

"You gonna invite me in or what?"

"This is a surprise," said Atticus to the man that he'd given the bird to the last time they'd seen each other. In fact, it was a double bird. It would have been more if Atticus had the power of Ganesha. "I wasn't expecting… Well, I never thought I'd ever see you again.

"So what the fuck?"

"Uh… what do you mean?" Atticus was reeling. Chuck Denning was a burly man, and the threat of physical violence was so imminent Atticus could almost feel the punch in his guts. The wind had already left him.

"I'm still on the fucking doorstep, aren't I?"

"Sure. Well, come in." Atticus wanted to get Denning into his office so that he could seat himself behind his desk and have Chuck in his visitor's chair. In that monster office chair he'd have nothing to fear from Chuck.

"Where's the shitter?" he asked as Atticus led him towards the study.

He was hoping that Chuck's visit to the toilet would be the brief kind but it wasn't. After about five minutes Denning emerged holding his belly. "Sorry, mate. Had some curry last night that didn't agree with me."

"Well, let's go to my study. I've had my daughter-in-law living in here and it's still more a nursery room than a lounge. What's he — my grandson-in-law? Makes the whole in-law thing seem silly, doesn't it?"

Atticus felt nervous. He always felt discombobulated when Denning was around. There was no explanation for it. He felt it with no-one else. It wasn't physical intimidation. It was a different kind of belligerence, and if Atticus was honest with himself, there was this need to turn Chuck around in his hostile opinion of Atticus.

"So this is my study," Atticus said leading him to the doorway, but Chuck said he needed water so they walked to the kitchen.

"Maybe I should explain m'self," said Chuck after drinking the glass and sighing like he'd knocked back a cold bottle of beer. But he didn't explain.

He saw the bowl of fruit on the kitchen table. He took an apple and didn't wash it before getting into it with a horse-size bite.

"That's still got the sticker on it." Atticus pointed out but Denning just looked at Atticus like he was a pansy. That word was written in his eyes. 'Pansy.' It was there quite often. In the break room with Chuck over the two decades they'd known each other, it'd always been there. This brooding silence that sapped the strength from Atticus and that word at the centre of it all.

Around a mouthful, gazing out the kitchen window into the mysteries of human weakness, Chuck said, "Shit." He didn't elucidate. After a few more horse-size bites, he said, "I've seen better days. I'll tell you that for something."

"For nothing," Atticus said before he could stop himself.

"What?"

"Tell you that for nothing."

"Tell me what?"

"Doesn't matter. Just enjoy your apple, please."

Chuck Denning didn't need an invitation. He continued to eat his apple—the core and seeds went down the hatch as well. Even the little bit of branch. "That's the problem with you, O'Neill. You start in on something and then you let the fucker go halfway through," Denning said, as he rummaged through the fruit bowl. He picked out a kiwifruit.

Atticus got up to give him a knife and a plate. Also the teaspoon he would need to dig out the fruit but Denning had already started eating the kiwi fruit like he had the apple, furry brown skin and all.

"What are you doing?" Atticus asked.

"Don't be a tight arse, mate."

"Please tell me you take the skin off a banana."

"Don't be a fucking idiot your whole life, O'Neill." From anyone else Atticus would have fired up but with Denning he could do nothing but allow it to pass and wait for the silence to settle. The truth was that he admired the way Chuck just ate a damned apple whole. The way a kiwifruit wasn't a messy, fiddly little thing, barely worth the trouble.

"I'm thinking about retirement," Denning said. "That's what I've been thinking about. That's why I'm here. I wanted to see how you're going."

A downcast Denning poured himself another glass of water from the tap. "I been working my whole fucking life mate. Since I was knee high to a fucken cockroach. Don't even do holidays. But isn't it bullshit, just going on and on until you drop? I'll be like one of those rattlers we used to drive that gets pulled off after how many fucking years because you couldn't rely on the brakes any more."

Chuck washed out his glass with a bit of water and put it back onto Atticus's dish rack to dry. "I'm the fucking W-class. That's me. Just keep going on until I crash. Or just the one last route. Up and down Chapel Street. Fucking up and down. Is that what I'm supposed to do? Fuck that."

After giving it some more thought, Denning reiterated, "Fuck that!"

"Let's talk about it in the study. I'll show you what I've been doing with my retirement."

"Sure." Chuck Denning was distracted by further stomach pains. He said he needed to go back to the toilet for a while. He hobbled out of the kitchen holding his belly again.

April was calling for Atticus from outside, to come help her with the pram and the shopping, and a hungry Dylan screaming for milk. As so often, when she was forced to babysit, it was a sudden whirlwind of catastrophe and mayhem, for minutes, until she was sitting quietly on the couch feeding the closed-eyed little ball of contentment. She whispered to Atticus that Richard had to gone out to Warrnambool to bring back Barbette.

Atticus went looking for Chuck Denning but he wasn't in the kitchen and he wasn't in the toilet or bathroom. He was in the study and was not sitting in the visitor's chair. He was sitting in Atticus's monster office chair and he looked comfortable. He was reading the screenplay and didn't seem to notice Atticus standing in the doorway—trembling with fury.

All of those many years of silent dismissal from Chuck Denning began boiling and seething up into his throat with a furious bile and there'd be no accounting for what was about to break loose from Atticus.

Chuck Denning looked up from a page of *Death By A Thousand Cuts*, with a surprised smile and said, "Not bad, mate." He threw the pages back onto the desk like yesterday's fish'n'chips but he nodded at them like he meant it. "Not bad at all."

And all Atticus could say to that was, "Really?" He moved to the old kitchen chair and sat down. Atticus cleared his throat and asked, "So… you thought it was good?"

A GREEN LIGHT

There was a small child with a dinosaur t-shirt pressing his face against the cold early morning glass to see a Qantas flight carve a groove into the dawn-smeared clouds above. The first thing the boy had shown Atticus was a baby lizard he kept in a large wooden pencil case.

The kid waved at Atticus when he left the warm taxi, not yet aware that men like Atticus didn't matter at all. That there was no point in waving good-bye to a taxi driver. Atticus didn't wave back. He lifted his head the slightest millimetre and offered a vague smile.

He'd had a brief nap in his taxi, and his head had filled with the infinite sounds of jets, airplanes from around the world coming in and rising up into the air, all that gigantic metal rising and falling like a controlled storm of leaves from a tree so vast the moon and sun were fruits hanging from a nearby branch.

A taxi driver beeped and shouted from behind him in the taxi ranks, and he killed the dream but Atticus didn't want to forget what he realised was an epiphany.

The aircraft could look so forlorn in every day life, lifting up into the sky like clumsy metal birds climbing with heavy wings. Such a colossal effort when for all other things avian, it was a simple grace achieved, even for the youngest duckling taking to the air for the first time. And the sound of those jets didn't often sound infinite and suggest the vast reaches of travel but the drill of noise it was almost impossible to entirely escape from anywhere in Melbourne or its suburbs.

He picked up a fare at the airport and drove away. He preferred his vision to the idea of life as nothing but movement and noise—useless and meaningless. He'd been driving to and from the airport for weeks, searching for his epiphany.

The drive to Melbourne airport had become like a new tram route for Atticus. There was good money in it but he'd discovered that he enjoyed hearing and seeing those immense jet engines lifting tons of polished metal, filled with all those expectant lives, into the air and landing majestically again. Rising and settling all around him. He leaned over his steering wheel and understood how that child with the dinosaur t-shirt felt. Atticus looked up through his windscreen with his mouth open, astounded by a world that could unfold landscapes, oceans and skies like maps anyone was allowed to buy.

The fare in the back of his taxi was distracting Atticus. The woman spoke on her mobile without pause. One call after another. Three different people in the ten minutes of the trip so far. There'd be no good-bye waves from her when they got to the Park Hyatt — her hotel of choice. He'd be lucky if she said a word to him outside of 'How much?'

He turned up his music despite the woman signalling him in the rear-view mirror to turn down the noise. It was great having music as he drove. He'd been buying a good collection of CDs by performers like Sting, Sade and Springsteen. It was a novelty to be able to listen to music as he did his job. The trams were filled with street noise, the whine and screech of metal wheels on steel rails, the electric clap and spark of contact with the overhead wiring, and the inane noises of people. He liked the song by Sting called *It's Probably Me*, and when it was finished he pressed the button that skipped it back and replayed it.

"Do you mind?" asked the passenger behind him.

She had her hand over her receiver and had lent through the gap to look at the side of Atticus's face.

"What about you minding? Or should I listen to your endless telephone conversations?" Atticus turned it down the slightest bit. The woman called him a jerk-off in an accent almost American but still mostly Australian. At a guess he would have said she'd been in the US the last ten years. It appalled Atticus that she repeatedly said Mel-Born instead of Mel-b'n. She can't have been gone that long that she'd forgotten how Australians pronounced the name of the greatest city in her country.

Atticus's mobile beeped to tell him he had a text message. It was April informing him that her eldest sister June, and her sister's friend Anais, would be coming to the opening of *Neighbours, The Musical*, after all. June was getting old and wasn't sure whether she wanted to be out that late, and Anais had been sick, and there was no way one would go without the other. It was a relief to April that the whole family would be coming to Barbette's big show. The text went on to list a few items Atticus could pick up from the supermarket on his way home. He switched his phone off before reading through them all.

Barbette had already had success touring the show throughout the UK and this was a return 'by popular demand' rather than an opening night, but it would be entertaining. There was something wonderful about seeing someone you knew well, out on a big stage, singing her heart out. There wasn't a performance that he didn't shed a tear. She was a lovely dancer and a truly memorable Daphne of Ramsay Street.

With the money Barbette had made she funded the relocation of the bakery into Brighton, and that was working out well for Dicky and Dylan. *The Baker of Brighton*. That's what they called the business and Barbette was happy to stay there when she was in Melbourne. They were some kind of family again but Barbette had never been the same after she came out of that acting academy out in Warrnambool.

A person really could have stars in their eyes, and it could be almost as serious a condition as a type of schizophrenia. Barbette couldn't speak of anything else anymore outside of theatre and film, other actors and scripts.

The woman in the back seat had just about as many stars in her eyes as did Barbette. For twenty minutes the conversation had revolved around a film she wanted to make but one she didn't want to do with the actor the film came attached with. It seemed clear, to Atticus at least, that the actor was far more integral to the project than the director in his back seat. Atticus debated whether he should mention his celebrity daughter-in-law but he didn't know who Harboiled Jean Sommerway was, why she was called that, or what made her so unappealing to the director, or appealing to the producers and studio execs on the other end of the phone. Was she really as mental as it seemed the director believed and was that even relevant to the performance she could turn in?

He tuned out and listened to Sting again. Sting was singing *Why Should I Cry For You?* by the time he was crossing Princes Highway.

"Don't I know you?" the woman said from the back seat.

"Excuse me?" he said to her reflection in the rear-view mirror.

"I fucking know you."

She leaned into the space between the front seats again and looked at the side of his face. "What happened to the rat's tail?"

"It was a ponytail." He grimaced into his side mirror as he negotiated a lane change. "I got rid of it."

"I knew I fucking knew you. You were the tram driver on the 96 for years. You always had this look about you, like it was fucking beneath you. But you always waited for me if I was running up to the stop to catch you. I had people shut tram doors in my face but you'd always wait. And that fucking rat's tail. Fucking hilarious!" He could feel her smile on his face it was so close to him. "So it's taxis now, hey? Is that where tram drivers go to die? Driving cabs around the city. Or is this moving up in the world?"

"It's just moving. Rising and falling like those planes. Like breathing. Don't get a choice most of the time."

She wasn't really listening. "And what about that fucking conductor? The one that whistled. The way that mother fucker whistled, man. Brought tears to my eyes once, I swear to fucking God! Do you remember that guy?"

"Do I remember him?"

He looked over his shoulder at her for the first time, and she didn't move away when they were within kissing distance from each other's faces. Atticus turned back to the traffic.

He turned Sting off. He cleared his throat and said, "I wrote a screenplay about him. About the trams in those days. About driving those routes through Melbourne. About all of that. So many stories to tell you'd hardly believe it. It's called *Off The Rails*. Though that can be changed. There's probably a better title for it."

Of course, Atticus hadn't actually written it but he knew he could write it. The tram driver wouldn't be him. It was Chuck Denning. The man who ate kiwi fruits whole. Who went on 'mule breaks' and told people things for 'something.' Atticus knew he had never done an interesting thing in his life outside of stealing a massive office chair from a truck that he'd been asked to look after, for a minute, as its driver went to use a public toilet Atticus had directed him to. Because Atticus was old enough to know better and he looked trustworthy and the driver was really having a terrible bowel crisis. So Atticus had never done anything of note but he'd seen interesting things and he remembered all of them. All Atticus had ever been waiting for in his life was a green light.

152

"Well, what the fuck? Tell me about this fucking screenplay."

They were still within kissing distance but the director didn't move away. They drove into Melbourne along the gleaming metal rails. Rails that wound through and around the city's heart. Threading along so many of its streets like flashing silver ribbons binding the whole city into a permanent gift to its people.

"*The Rattler*," he said. "That's a better title." He leaned back into the sheet of wooden beads April had bought for his car seat a few days ago.

"Okay. So it starts with a tram full of show dogs bound for a primary school recently burned to the ground. There are dogs with brightly coloured ribbons and sparkling tiaras all over the place — barking their fucking heads off."

Acknowledgements

Stories in this book have been published or recorded, sometimes in slightly different versions, as follows:

The Rattler , shortlisted for Melbourne Lord Mayor's Awards 2009. Highly Commended certificate for 3 Hour Book (novella) category
The Coultas Kid, Wet Ink Issue #16, 2009
Ducks, Etchings Issue #8, 2009
Some Kind of Blues, Quadrant April Issue, 2009
Prayers for Cracks in the Concrete, Going Down Swinging Issue #29, 2009
Jiggling the Molecules, Page Seventeen, Issue # 8, 2010
I Wanna Be Murakami, Stop Drop and Roll Issue #2, 2010
The Amsterdam Keyhole, Blue Crow Issue #1, 2010
The Frame, 21D Issue #2 – Street, 2011
The Ink on Her Lips, Etchings, Issue #10, 2011
Serpentine Red, Red Leaves, Issue #2, 2011
B O M B S, miniPAN (single story issue), 2011
Back When Jean-Michel Basquiat Was My Best Friend, PAN, Issue #2, 2011

About the artists

Miles Allinson
(graphics on pp 14, 25, 46, 60, 96, 104)

Miles is an artist and writer. He lives in Melbourne and blogs at:
mrcurly.blogspot.com

Maxine Beneba Clarke
(graphic on p.113)

Maxine is a Melbourne based West Indian-Australian writer
and artist. Her most recent book is the poetry collection
Gill Scott Heron is on Parole (Picaro Press, 2010). She has
been a cover designer for Overland Literary Journal and her
illustrations have also appeared in Unusual Works, Overland
Literary Journal Online, Verity La and on her own writing
blog at slamup.blogspot.com.

Also published by Spineless Wonders:

Unflinching realism...compelling and complex in equal measure.
The Australian

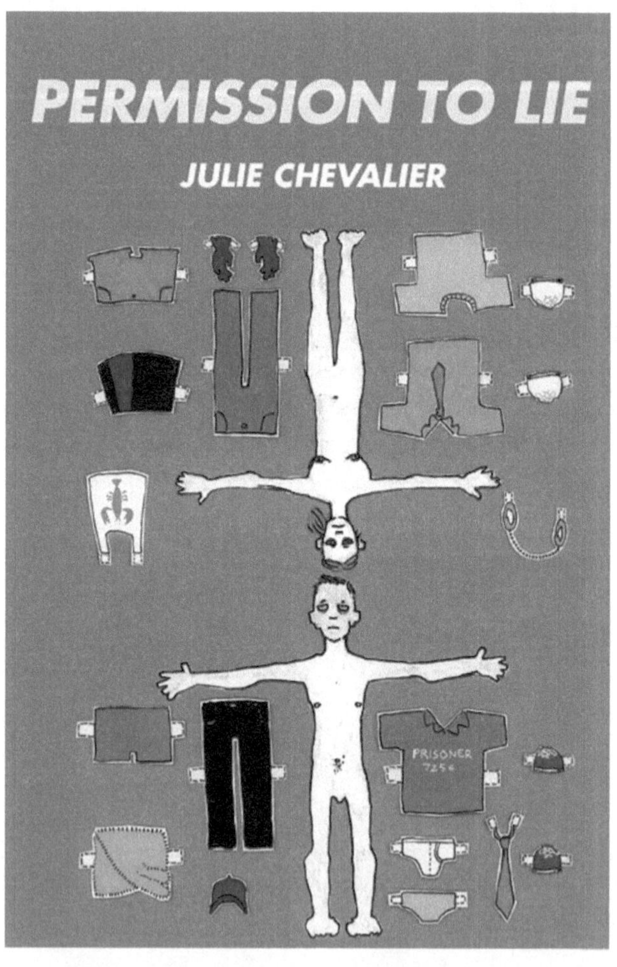

Permission To Lie
by Julie Chevalier

In this wonderfully diverse collection, Chevalier does not flinch from delving into some of the messier aspects of contemporary Australian culture, whether inside prisons, nudist camps or in cut-throat boardrooms.

Includes six pages of quirky illustrations by Paden Hunter.

> *'Holding together the extensive range of this collection is prose of a deceptive simplicity, taut, droll, hinting at greater depths, never giving too much away. A new voice in Australian fiction, wry, gritty, knowing and true.'*
> **Fiona McGregor**,
> author of Indelible Ink

Available from participating bookshops and online. For further information about where to purchase our print and ebooks, go to the Spineless Wonders website:

www.shortaustralianstories.com.au